Contrary Winds

A Novel of the American Revolution

USA Today best-selling author

Lea Wait

Sheepscot River Press
Post Office Box 225
Edgecomb, Maine 04556

ISBN 978-0-9964084-7-9 (print)
ISBN 978-0-9964084-9-3 (Kindle)

AUGUST, 1777

Chapter 1
Boothbay, Massachusetts (District of Maine)

"I cannot bear living in this place!" Rory Campbell threw himself down on the ground next to the stream where Sarah was washing clothes. "Men no older than I am are fighting for our freedom. I'm stuck in the middle of nowhere."

It was a hot, dry, summer, and the American Revolution was not going at all well.

Even people living in the wilderness of Massachusetts called the District of Maine, one hundred and fifty miles northeast of Boston, knew that. The British had seized New York City, and General Washington's army hadn't won a battle since January.

"Get up out of the dirt, Rory. Yer making more washing for me to do." Sarah brushed a strand of long hair off her face as she scrubbed his shirt with smooth rocks she'd collected at the shoreline. "How ever do ye manage to get yer clothes so filthy?"

"Chasing Perkins' pig. She'd gotten out of the town pen." Rory jumped up and kicked a stone into the stream. "I'm fourteen! I shouldn't be chasing pigs. I should be fighting for our new nation, as cousin Malcolm is, or at least standing guard in the Seacoast Defense, like Uncle and Hugh."

"Both the army and the militia require ye to be sixteen. Yer tall enough, as well I know from having to sew yer new breeches, but Mother will not forget what day ye were born. She'll never give her consent. Nor will Uncle."

Boothbay, an area of islands, coves, and peninsulas surrounding Townsend Harbor on the cold north Atlantic, had been settled by a few families from Scotland and Ireland in 1730. Now two dozen families lived there, most in small homes made of pine logs. Before the war they'd made a living from lumbering, and from the sea.

Boom! A cracking explosion broke the peace.

Boom! And then — boom! Three shots rang out from south of the field where Rory and Sarah were standing. Trees that once stood there had been felled for fuel, building homes, and trade.

Then the shots were echoed by another three to their north. And then by a third set of three, even further north, as the message was carried along the coastline.

"It's the alarm!" Rory picked up the basket of wet clothes and they ran back toward the shore. Toward home.

The shots meant a British ship had been sighted. It was the call to arms, directing every resident of Boothbay to go straight to their home and be accounted for. Then all able-bodied men sixteen and older would take their muskets, ammunition, and two days provisions, and meet at one of five meeting places to await orders.

Since the English had burned Falmouth, the largest city in the District of Maine, two years before, the British Navy had been raiding villages and trading posts along the coast, stealing muskets, gunpowder, ammunition, and animals to use as food for their soldiers and sailors. Villages in Maine sent men to fight in the Continental Army knowing their absence would leave families with few defenses in the face of this constant harassment.

The Campbell family had compromised: their oldest son, Malcolm, had enlisted, while twenty-year-old Hugh and his father had stayed, serving in the Seacoast Defense. They weren't cowards. Day and night, men in the Defense took their turns standing along the cliffs and shores of Maine, ready to sound the alarm when an English ship was sighted. As one of them had just done.

In truth, for many men in Boothbay there was little else to be done in 1777.

English soldiers and sailors had stolen their livelihoods.

They'd taken or destroyed most of the small boats used for fishing and transportation on the coast, leaving Mainers isolated and without means to fish the North Atlantic. And since colonists had long since cut down forests near the coast, no wildlife remained to be hunted for meat.

Before the war most food had come from Boston in trade for timber for masts, shingles and fuel. Now there were no large vessels, and therefore no way to reach Boston.

Only a few small boats remained in Boothbay, all hidden deep in the narrow twists and turns of Campbell's Cove. The half-dozen animals the English hadn't found were near the town's small garrison, built after the battles of Lexington and Concord and hidden behind a stone wall above the cove where three-foot-thick mortared walls of field stones surrounded a small cannon, cannon balls, and extra ammunition. The stone walls and roof were intended to keep the gunpowder dry, although dampness hadn't been a problem in this summer of drought.

Those hidden boats were Boothbay's only way to reach other towns. This far east, seas and rivers were roads. In only a few places along the coast did ancient Abenaki or Penobscot trails link European settlements.

Uncle Andra was already loading his musket when Rory and Sarah reached home. Mother was putting a few dried wild apples into a basket with the last of the bacon as provisions for the men of the Defense.

"Where's Hugh?" asked Uncle Andra, nodding at Rory and Sarah, as though they were chickens to be counted.

"He went down to the mud flat to dig clams," said Mother. "He would've heard the alarm. He'll be with us soon enough."

"The flat's in sight of the harbor. Let's hope Hugh heard the alarm or saw the ships before they saw him." Uncle Andra pulled on his worn brown jacket and hat, anxious to be on his way.

"Please, may I go with you and Hugh this time? Ye know I can shoot. And I'll be fifteen in six months!" Rory looked longingly at the musket his uncle was holding, and then at his own, still hanging on the wall. In Scotland he'd had no use for a weapon, but one of the first skills he'd learned in this new country was how to handle a gun.

"Rory, yer too young, and yer not ready. We've talked this through many times. Stay and protect yer mother and sister. Deal with yer fears and nightmares before ye find yourself in the middle of new ones." Uncle Andra turned toward the door.

Rory's cheeks turned scarlet as an English soldier's coat. In their small house his nightmares couldn't be secret, but they were private.

"Yer not my Da, to be telling me what to do. I know the English. And fighting them's what I want to do!"

Before his uncle could respond the door banged open and Hugh stomped in, his arms and legs covered with the heavy black mud of the flats, leaving footprints across the clean pine floor. He dropped a small sack of clams on the table. "Food for you that'll be staying here," he said, patting Sarah's head with his muddy hand. She wiped the smelly muck off her hair and made a face at him behind his back.

Her mother frowned at her. "Thank you, Hugh. Clams will make for good eating. Get your boots on, then, and get along. Our hearts go with ye."

Uncle Andra frowned at Rory. "Lad, ye'll be a man soon enough, and ready to do what ye must. But for now I'm taking yer Da's place, and I'm saying what he would have. Yer not ready, and until ye are, ye'll stay here and help take care of our home and our women."

The two men ran out, and down the path to their assigned station at Andrew McFarland's home. They might be back in an hour, or perhaps not for a day or two.

Rory said nothing, but took his musket from its place on the wall.

Last month young Caleb Brewer, down to Ocean Point, had stood in front of his house and fired a gun toward an English vessel rounding the point, headed for Boothbay. The ship had fired back.

It had taken his mother many days to scrub Caleb's blood off the clapboards of his house. He was now down in the burying ground next to the church.

Even Rory knew that was not the kind of excitement he longed for.

Chapter 2
News!

Mother and Rory and Sarah sat up all night, dozing, and sleeping in their clothes. Rory had loaded his musket and put it on the table near the door, on the chance he should have to use it.

The first time they'd heard the alarm was shortly after they'd arrived from Scotland the summer before. They'd sat up all night then, too, scared and keeping each other from thinking about what might be happening by singing songs from the old country, and reminding each other of their life in Scotland. But stories of life before Da and Johnnie had died saddened them all, and when he'd returned, Uncle had sternly cautioned them to keep silent, in case any English soldiers should come ashore and their voices guide the enemy to their door.

Now they knew to sit silently, keeping their thoughts and fears and prayers to themselves. And to God.

Uncle Andra and Hugh returned soon after daybreak. "It was Admiral Collier's vessels again," Uncle Andra reported. "They sailed southwest, toward the Kennebec. Thank the good Lord they didn't try to land here. I hope our friends up the coast will be as lucky as we were this time."

"We heard news at the McFarlands'," said Hugh. "One of the lads from over to Southport managed to get up river to Wiscasset last week."

"Aye?" said Mother. News was rare, and welcome.

"A family there received a letter from a man who enlisted in March with our Malcolm. When the letter was written, in early May, Colonel Francis' regiment was at Fort Ticonderoga."

"Where is that? Were they fighting?" asked Rory.

"Not as yet, but English troops were gathering north of there, in Canada," said Uncle Andra. "Ticonderoga is in New York, north of the Hudson River, at the very southern part of Lake Champlain."

"But everyone was still safe?" Mother had sat down, her hands in her lap.

"So it sounded. At least we know where our boy was then. And Francis' regiment was serving under General St. Clair – a Scotsman born, and known to be a fair and good man."

"But it's over two months since that note was penned. Battles may have been fought and won – or lost – since then," Mother added quietly. "Let us pray our brave Maine boys are still well and as full of hope as when they left their homes. And that they come back to us soon."

"Malcolm signed up to serve until the war ended," Uncle Andra reminded her.

"Then let us hope it ends soon," said Mother.

Rory closed his fists tightly. He didn't want Malcolm to be hurt; he wanted him to come home. But he didn't want the war to be over before he'd had his chance to be a part of it.

"And then," said Hugh, "We heard something else, perhaps of interest to Miss Sarah." He reached out and tweaked her ear.

"Hugh," Uncle Andra admonished, "That matter had best be discussed by Sarah's mother and I before it is shared with the lass."

"I'm almost thirteen years old," said Sarah. "I can hear whatever

9

it is concerns me." She stood up and looked from Uncle to Hugh to Mother and then back to her uncle. "So, what was said?"

"Go ahead, Andra," said Mother. "I trust whatever it is she'll treat as a woman would." She put her hand on Sarah's shoulder.

Sarah sat down, but leaned forward so she wouldn't miss anything.

"Last year, when ye were on yer way here from Scotland, ye stopped in Nova Scotia for a time, until the seas were clear enough for yer vessel to get through and arrive safely," said Uncle Andra.

"Aye, we did," said Mother. "We stayed at a small boarding house in Halifax with others in the same predicament."

"Do ye remember a Mr. and Mrs. Biddle? Not young people, I believe."

"I do," replied Mother, nodding. "Mrs. Biddle's cousin was a minister in Maine, and she and Mr. Biddle were traveling to meet him. He'd prepared a home for them in Wiscasset, as I remember."

"She was the fat old lady," said Sarah. "The one who smelled of too much lavender water."

"Sarah!" said Mother.

Hugh and Rory burst out laughing, and even Mother and Uncle smiled.

"Sarah!" said Mother. "You must not say such things! But, aye, I do believe we're remembering the same Mrs. Biddle."

"Well, it seems Mrs. Biddle has lost her husband. He died of a fever last month."

"The poor woman," said Mother. "All alone, and in a new country as well."

"She's having a hard time of it. She would like to return to England, but, of course, that is not easy to arrange. It seems, Sarah, that she also remembers you from the boarding house, and wonders if you would like to go and live with her for a while," said Uncle

Chapter 3
Decisions Made

"Yer really going?" Rory said. He and Sarah stood in the high grasses and sea lavender, looking out at the sea. Mudflats stretched in front of them like a dark mantle embroidered with seaweed and bleached wood brought in by the tide and broken clam and mussel shells dropped by hungry herring gulls. "Yer going to keep house for that fat old lady? I didn't think you'd be brave enough to leave home on yer own!"

"Most likely I'll only be gone the summer."

"And I'll still be here." Rory kicked a stone on the shore so hard it almost reached the receding waters.

"I won't be far away. Wiscasset is just upriver," said Sarah. "I do wish it were you going, Rory. Yer the one who should be leaving home first. But it's not yer kind of adventure. I won't be fighting British soldiers! Perhaps Uncle will relent and let you join the Seacoast Defense."

"More likely he'll tell me again to wait until I'm sixteen, as he always does," said Rory. "So it's tomorrow yer leaving, fer sure?"

Sarah nodded. "Jonathan Decker has a small skiff. He's taking mail and the gunpowder Boothbay folks have made to Wiscasset on the incoming tide tomorrow morning. I'm going with him."

Rory turned slowly toward her. "Just you and Jonathan?"

"Aye; I believe so."

"Then perhaps Jonathan could use some help with his skiff. My sister should be accompanied to Wiscasset by her brother. And that gunpowder should have more than one man protecting it!" Rory turned and strode back up the hill toward home.

Chapter 4
Sheepscot River Journey

Rory, Sarah, and Jonathan left before sunrise in Jonathan's small wooden skiff. Their cargo included Sarah's small bundle of clothing and a tin water-tight box of gunpowder, the result of several months' work by the townspeople of Boothbay. They had replenished their own supply, which was tightly held and rationed, and the rest would now be on its way to the Continental Army.

Rowing twelve miles upriver, even with an incoming tide, was no small task, but British raids had left Boothbay no sailing vessels.

They pushed off in the soft darkness before dawn, when the air was still cool and they'd also have the least chance of being seen. Jonathan and Rory each took an oar. Sarah sat in the prow as lookout.

"We won't have to watch for Admiral Collier's ships; they sailed past our harbor three days ago," Rory pointed out as he lifted his oar and bent forward, pushing it down hard, then pulling it back through the dark waters.

"True enough. But the Admiral isn't the only Brit who means us harm. Smaller brigs and sloops belonging to Tories who're trying to establish themselves down east of here, or even in Nova Scotia, have been burning houses and plundering whatever food they can find up and down the coast. With trade stopped, everyone's in need of supplies. And gunpowder is valued by both armies."

"I didn't realize British sympathizers were everywhere along the northern coast," said Sarah quietly.

"No doubt your uncle felt you didn't need to know," Jonathan said. "Women shouldn't have to worry about such things."

"That explains why the Seacoast Defense stands guard twenty-four hours a day, even when they know Admiral Collier, or Captain Mowatt, or the other British commanders, are not nearby," said Rory. "Uncle's always said it was just a precaution."

"For sure it's that. It's not unheard of for a vessel to pass a town by, and then return within hours, make landfall, and attack," said Jonathan.

"The war is not only far away, where battles are being fought. It's here, too. There's almost no one we can trust," said Sarah, quietly.

Jonathan grinned. "You can trust me, Sarah Campbell. Trust me to get you to Wiscasset. But when you get there you'll find not all folks are patriots, like those in Boothbay. Watch your tongue until you know who you're talking to."

"You mean there are spies?"

"Perhaps. For sure there are Tories. Merchants like Abiel Wood, whose money was made in trade with England, and who has deep loyalties there. Now he's trading with men in Nova Scotia when he can, and has even moved his family there, as have others who don't feel safe in a town where their loyalties are questioned."

While they talked the young men rowed the small boat around the northern tip of Southport Island, and headed up the Sheepscot River with the tide, weaving their way among the many small islands in the river.

Tall white pines, the trees valued most for masts by both Americans and the French and English they'd traded with before the war, lined the river banks. In some areas the trees had been felled for lumber or fuel. Land there was covered by rocks and bramble-covered stumps.

An osprey cried and soared far overhead. Rory kept his eyes on the shoreline, taking note when he saw a willow tree, hoping he could find it in the future when they needed to make more charcoal for gunpowder.

Sarah touched the boys' shoulders and silently pointed at a dark granite ledge exposed by the tide. Dozing harbor seals looked up at them in interest as the small boat passed them. One young seal plunged into the river and swam after them until he lost interest and returned to the ledge.

"Wouldn't it be faster if we rowed up the channel?" asked Rory. His palms were already blistered by the oar. "The currents would carry us further, and we'd be on a more direct route. Going around all these islands is taking us much longer."

"It's safer this way," replied Jonathan. "Most vessels sailing up or down the river will take the more obvious, deep water route. They won't be as apt to see us here, and even if they did, it would be easier for us to hide among the inlets and coves on the islands. Not to mention that we can row in waters where larger vessels would run aground on rocks or mud."

Rory nodded.

The sun had been high for hours when they reached the northern end of Jeremy Squam Island and could see the rooftops of Wiscasset. Rory's hands were bloodied with broken blisters, and the muscles in his back and thighs ached. Currents in the deep tidal river ran strong.

"I can take both oars for the last stretch, if you like," Jonathan volunteered. "When weather permits I make this trip once or twice a month. My hands are callused with rowing."

Rory shook his head. He'd said he'd help, and he'd do it.

Despite the bottle of spring water Mother had given them, all three were thirsty and drenched with sweat in the hot mid-day sun.

"We'll return on tomorrow afternoon's tide," said Jonathan. "That will give me time to make plans with friends, and for you to see your sister well placed." They steered around the northern tip of Jeremy Squam Island. Wiscasset lay just ahead of them across the river.

Two large vessels were in Wiscasset's harbor. They appeared to be at anchor, their sails still being furled.

"How did they get by us?" Sarah whispered.

"Who are they?" asked Rory.

The same question was on all three of their minds: were the ships friends or foes?

Sarah crouched down on the floor of the skiff and took a short gown, a shawl, and an apron out of her bag of clothing, leaving it almost empty.

"What are you doing?" asked Jonathan.

She slipped the short gown over her shoulders, put on her apron, and fastened her shawl around her shoulders.

"It's blazing hot out here already! You're dressed as though it's December!"

Sarah smiled as she carefully slipped the box of gunpowder inside her sack. It was a close fit, but the box was covered.

Spinning wheels and looms could replace clothing, although even that was becoming more difficult since there were few sheep now left in Maine. But battles could not be won without gunpowder.

Chapter 5
In Wiscasset

"The vessels must have come across the Sasanoa River from the Kennebec and been on the other side of Jeremy Squam Island," said Jonathan, "Or else we were dodging between islands, and missed seeing each other."

"I canna imagine a vessel the size of those would be interested in us," added Rory. "That one on the right is a full three-masted, square-rigged ship. That's the sort we came from Scotland on. The little sloop with only one mast couldn't sail across the Atlantic."

"Not many ships *or* sloops are left belonging to Americans. The British have seized all except the few that folks have managed to hide. I've even heard a few towns have sunk their own vessels, hoping to haul them up in happier days to come." Jonathan craned his neck to look. "I don't see the British flag. Usually that Union Jack is waving proudly, to show us how much stronger their navy is than ours."

"In truth it is," said Rory. "But they've had a few hundred years to build it."

"There's no gunfire or smoke," Sarah pointed out. "If British vessels are there, they don't appear to be fighting. And we're just young people. Yer taking me to Mrs. Biddle's home. I'll carry my sack. Why would anyone bother a young lass carrying personal clothing?"

The boys looked at each other and grinned.

"You've got a smart sister, Rory," said Jonathan.

"And if there should be trouble, perhaps we could help. I wish I'd brought my musket!" Rory added.

Jonathan looked from one to the other of his passengers. "It's decided then. We'll go on to Wiscasset."

He and Rory picked up the oars and bent to their task, while Sarah focused on the view across the river.

In more peaceful times Wiscasset's harbor was no doubt a busy one. Seven long wharves led from the shore out into the channel, providing enough space for dozens of sailing vessels to be docked so even shifting tides wouldn't strand them on mudflats. But except for the two large vessels, only a few rowboats and skiffs were now in the wide harbor.

Beyond the wharves, four streets of houses stretched on a gently sloping hill topped by a white-washed church. It wasn't a large bustling town like Falkirk, their home in Scotland, but it was more organized than the scattered homes that made up the settlement of Boothbay. Which house would she be living in? Sarah leaned forward and tried to see everything at once.

Three shipyards bordered the long wharves, but the yards were now empty, and the sail lofts, mercantile store, and tannery near them were also deserted. There was no need for them without vessels to equip.

Jonathan and Rory brought the skiff about, to a site near a small wharf on the land side of Kingsbury's Ship Yard. Like the others, it was closed and empty. Pulling the skiff up so it was partially on dry land, they tied it to a tree.

The tide was now high. When it turned the skiff would be completely on dry land.

"Do you know where Mrs. Biddle lives?" asked Jonathan, turning to Sarah.

She shook her head. "No."

Several young men about Jonathan's age gathered near them on the street. Jonathan nodded at one particularly lanky fellow wearing a bright blue waistcoat. "What's the news, Ben? Are the vessels in the harbor ours or theirs?"

"Ours. Captain Proctor's brought the *Gruel* here by order of the Provincial Board of War. She's out of Marblehead. Sailed in June, but had to stop in Falmouth for repairs."

"Why bring her here, with British ships watching our coast so closely?" asked Jonathan.

"On order of Doctor Benjamin Franklin, our country's ambassador to the French court. We're to load her with white pine masts, and then sail her to France, just as we did before the war, for the French Navy. Word is it's a bribe. Dr. Franklin's trying to get the French to join with us and fight against the English."

Jonathan whistled. "Having the French Navy on our side would indeed be a help! But how does Captain Proctor think he can hide a ship that size in Wiscasset until she's filled with masts, and then just sail her past the English?"

"He's taking a risk, for sure. But there's no gain without risk, they say." Ben shrugged.

"And the smaller vessel?"

"That's the *Martha*, to take mariners from the *Gruel* back to Falmouth. Only Captain Proctor and three of his men will be staying with the *Gruel*. Falmouth can't spare more men to spend the summer sitting in Wiscasset."

"Then there's much to talk about. Gather the other lads, Ben, and I'll be at the usual place at six. First I must show this young lady to Mrs. Biddle's residence." He turned back to Sarah. "Follow me." He hesitated a moment. "Let me carry that sack for you."

"Thank you, Jonathan." Sarah handed it to him, and Rory

followed them as Jonathan led them up a hill to their left, past a small garrison. Further down the dirt lane Jonathan knocked at a one-story white-washed house.

Mrs. Biddle opened the door. She was dressed in black, from her bonnet to her shoes, and was even wider than Sarah remembered.

"Ma'am," Jonathan said, tipping his hat, "Mrs. Biddle, you asked for Sarah Campbell from Boothbay, and I've brought her."

"Ohhhhh!" Mrs. Biddle reached out and pulled Sarah to her ample breast. The embrace almost took Sarah's breath away. After a moment or two of inhaling the lavender scent she'd remembered so clearly, Sarah slowly backed up. "It's very nice to see you again, Mrs. Biddle. My family and I were saddened to hear of Mr. Biddle's death."

Mrs. Biddle stood and nodded, putting a handkerchief edged with black lace to her eyes. "Thank you, my dear. It's been a difficult time for me. A very difficult time. I knew you would understand, since you and your mother lost your dear father in Scotland."

"Aye. We did," agreed Sarah. "I understand ye were looking for some help and companionship this summer."

"Of course, of course! That's precisely why I asked you to come!" Mrs. Biddle moved out of the doorway. "Please, come in! It's so wonderful to see someone who reminds me of home! And Rory has grown so much!"

Jonathan removed the gunpowder box from Sarah's bag, handed the almost empty bag to her, and tipped his hat before heading down the street.

"Sarah, I'm going to spend some time looking at the town. I'll be back to see you later, since Jonathan won't be leaving until tomorrow." Rory looked after Jonathan's departing figure.

Sarah had no time to respond, as Mrs. Biddle nodded at swept her into the house. "My dear girl, you must be hungry and thirsty, and of course, there is so little to eat and drink in this dreadful country. Because of this impossible war everything has been at sixes and sevens since we left England. But I shall find something for you, nevertheless."

The door closed behind her.

Sarah was in her new place of residence.

And Rory was on his own in Wiscasset.

Chapter 6
A Dangerous Opportunity

After the door closed, Rory stood for a minute. Then he grinned. Here, indeed, was adventure. He was alone, in a new place, with no need to think of returning to Boothbay until the next day. Free!

But what to do with this freedom? Jonathan and the box of gunpowder had already disappeared.

Rory walked further down the hard dirt lane until he found the main street of Wiscasset. To his left the church stood, on top of a slight hill. Below it was a rectangular green marked as a training field for soldiers, although no militia units were drilling today. Instead, a dozen small boys were lined up on one side of the field, sticks held on their shoulders the way their fathers or older brothers held muskets. Proudly they marched from one side of the field to the other, turned right, then left, and marched back.

How long would the war go on, Rory wondered. Would these boys, some no older than four or five, someday be soldiers like the ones they were imitating?

Fourteen had to be the worst age of all: too young to be a soldier, and too old to be a child.

Sheep were openly grazing in a fenced area to the north. Animals in Wiscasset must not have to be as hidden as those at the coast.

A row of commercial buildings lay between the training field and the river, but only two seemed busy. The doors and shutters of a two-story wood-shingled building labeled "Whittier's Tavern" were propped open in the heat; loud male voices inside could occasionally be heard in the quiet street. Further down the hill, nearer the waterfront, small clusters of women stood near Brackett's Store.

From a distance came the clear sound of a sledge hammer on an anvil. Blacksmiths kept busy even in wartime. Lead balls of all sizes, for cannons and muskets, would have to be cast, portable cooking utensils were essential for soldiers, and farms and kitchens on the home front had to be maintained.

Uncle Andra had given Malcolm a musket when he enlisted, and had also bought him a leather cartridge box and wooden canteen, a knife, a horn cup and powder horn, and a wooden trencher, "so he'd have some decent way of eating." Mother'd even insisted on Uncle's supplying Malcolm with a small iron griddle. She'd heard of soldiers who'd resorted to cooking on stones heated in open fires.

Rory walked down to the waterfront and looked out at the wharves, most empty but for the two vessels he'd seen as they'd entered the harbor. Where were the vessels which had once sailed from this port? Had the English seized them, or had they stayed at foreign ports, or at ports in states the English did not control?

Then he saw a familiar figure ahead of him.

"Jonathan, wait!" He ran to catch up.

The older boy hesitated, but turned. "I thought you were with your sister, Rory."

"I left her with Mrs. Biddle. I wanted to see Wiscasset." He looked at Jonathan's hands. "Ye no longer have the gunpowder."

"You can't follow me, Rory. I have business here. I've already turned the gunpowder over to Colonel Jones, head of the Wiscasset militia. He'll store it until there's an opportunity to transport it to our troops." Jonathan stood a bit taller. "What I'm doing is important for the war effort. Why don't you go and be with your sister and Mrs. Biddle? I don't want you in any danger."

"I'm not a child," said Rory. "I can hold my tongue, and I can shoot." He lowered his voice and glanced around to make certain no one else was listening. "If yer doing something to aid the war, perhaps I can be of help."

Jonathan took Rory's arm and guided him to the side of Water Street, next to one of the empty sail lofts. He spoke softly. "You must swear, on your honor, not to tell anyone."

"Aye. I do swear!" Rory whispered.

"I carry messages between officers of the Seacoast Defense in Boothbay and the militia in Wiscasset. When I hear Tories speaking of British activities, I make sure our side knows about them too."

"Ye spy on the Tories and those who would prevent the Revolution from succeeding?" Rory asked. He kept his voice low, but his face flushed with excitement.

"To be a true patriot you must look sharp. There are some who don't want the colonies to form their own country. They're happy with being part of England. They may have family in England, like Mrs. Biddle; or they just don't want their world to change."

"But haven't most of those people left?" Uncle Andra and his cousins had talked of Tories leaving the District of Maine. "I thought those loyal to the crown had formed regiments to fight with the English forces and moved their families back to England, or to Canada."

"That's true enough, so far as it goes. In the early days of the war many Tories here had access to ships, and they left. But some Tories have neither money nor inclination to leave. They've stayed, believing we patriots will lose. They help the British forces by telling them what our army and militias are planning."

Chapter 7
Mrs. Biddle

Mrs. Biddle's kitchen was small, but bright and immaculate. Despite the mid-day heat the fire in her large brick fireplace was crackling, and she had two iron kettles on the crane over the flames. Her oven must also have been full; the house smelled of baking bread.

Where had Mrs. Biddle gotten wheat or corn? In Boothbay they had not had grain in months.

Sarah realized she hadn't eaten all day.

"Dear, for now just put down your bag. Later I'll show you where everything is," said Mrs. Biddle, gesturing at a low bench next to a wide pine trestle table on which lay a Bible, a red teapot, and several pewter plates and mugs. "My dear cousin, the Reverend Jacob Bailey, prepared this house and everything in it for Mr. Biddle and me before we arrived from England last year. We'd hoped he'd be living closer to us. But his church is in Pownalborough, and there are no roads between here and there, only dirt trails marked with axe marks on trees. I can't be expected to walk fifteen miles on a trail like that, and there are no horses here, and certainly no carriages. Did you know that before you arrived, Sarah? No horses north of the Kennebec River, they tell me, because there are no roads safe for them to travel. No roads safe for a decent woman to travel, that's what I say. A far cry from life in England, where people are civilized. And would you like a cup of tea?"

"*Tea?*" Sarah asked in amazement. The colonies had not had tea since before 1773. The English had put a heavy tax on it, and the colonies had refused to pay. She had not had tea since she'd left Nova Scotia. Even if someone had tea hidden away, purchased before 1773, a true patriot would have long since thrown it out. No one would dare it be known he or she had used any goods that had come from Great Britain, or from any company connected with England. Even a newcomer on an isolated point in the wilds of the District of Maine knew that!

Mrs. Biddle lowered her voice. "Now, don't you be telling anyone. I brought some tea with me over that horrid ocean, and I don't mind saying I think it was an intelligent thing to do. I don't have much left, but you being a fellow countrywoman and this being such a time, with Mr. Biddle having gone to his rest and so forth ..." She took a pewter tea caddy from the brightly painted yellow cupboard, added a few tea leaves to the teapot on the table, and tilted one of the kettles to add hot water to it. "I usually keep my teapot on a high shelf, and just take it out for special occasions. If anyone sees it, I say it reminds me of home, and is a spot of color in a dreary place." She winked at Sarah. "Sometimes I put wildflowers in it, for show! But today I just had to take it out to remind me of home, and now I know why!"

Sarah swallowed hard. A patriot would never drink a cup of tea that taxes had been paid on. But she didn't want to insult Mrs. Biddle. And clearly no American taxes had been paid on *this* tea, if Mrs. Biddle had brought it with her. "One cup, then, Mrs. Biddle. But that is all. It's yer tea, and I won't be telling anyone about it. But no more for me after this." Sarah lowered her voice. "Some would have us tarred and feathered for having even a taste of tea."

Mrs. Biddle nodded. "Don't I know it. They did just that to a man over in Bath earlier this spring for keeping in touch with some friends he did business with in England." She shook her head. "These Americans, as they're calling themselves, are a rowdy bunch. Most of them too poor or uneducated to be successful in England, or whatever country they've escaped from, so they're here, doing as they please, and making all sorts of trouble for the king and all of us."

Sarah took a tiny sip of her tea, to make it last longer. "It's delicious." She wished Mother could taste it. Mother missed tea. And thank goodness Rory was not here. He would have had Mrs. Biddle arrested for even mentioning tea! "But ye know, Mrs. Biddle, we're not really countrywomen. I'm a Scotswoman." Sarah smoothed her worn blue skirt, thinking her dear father would have scolded and said she was just a wee lass putting on airs to say such a thing.

"I know it, girl. And if we were back in the British Isles you being Scots and me being English would mean a world of difference. But in this land, full of ragged fellows who defy kings, I keep thinking Scotland touches England, and that's closer than I'll get to home any time soon. My dear cousin is so far away and busy with his church and his correspondence and who knows what else that I hardly see him. And you and I shared that horrid voyage across the Atlantic, and that dreadful boarding house in Halifax. I'm so thankful your mother — how is your dear mother, by the way? — your mother could spare you to help me in my time of sorrow."

"Mother is very well, thank you," said Sarah. "Did you hear she married my Uncle Andra last winter?"

"It seems to me I did hear that," said Mrs. Biddle. "That was your dear father's brother, that you were traveling to stay with, wasn't it?"

Sarah nodded. "We lived with a neighbor of his, Mrs. Reed, until they were married. It was all very proper. He has two sons. Malcolm is in the 11th Massachusetts now, serving under Colonel Francis at

Fort Ticonderoga in New York State. Hugh is in the Seacoast Defense with Uncle Andra."

"Oh, this horrible war. I cannot understand why these people are not honored by being part of the British Empire. Instead, they're clamoring about and making speeches and it's impossible to get a decent pair of shoes in this country, and nigh impossible to get good beef or mutton," said Mrs. Biddle.

Sarah smiled to herself. Her own shoes were almost worn through, but, of course, without animals, there was no leather. "I've heard our soldiers are finding the absence of meat and shoe leather difficult."

"Well then, why don't they just stop their fighting, and settle down. Then they'd have plenty of time for raising crops and animals, and the tanners and shoemakers could get back to their trades and we could all enjoy a bit of peace." Mrs. Biddle raised her handkerchief to her eyes. "And I could find passage on a vessel home, and not be stuck in this outpost of humanity in the wilderness of Massachusetts!"

Sarah sipped her tea, wishing she had not declared she would have only one cup.

"Would you like a scone, Sarah?"

A scone! Sarah could only nod. Mother would say Mrs. Biddle was a bit of an odd duck, and Jonathan would likely call her a Tory, but she had somehow found flour and she had a bit of tea, and Sarah began to wonder if perhaps, just perhaps, she might also have some soap hidden away. Without animals there was no fat to make soap. Sarah hated washing with only water.

Strange vessels in the harbor, an old lady who had her own views on life, and a whole town full of new people to meet and places to explore. This summer of 1777 was looking more interesting every hour.

Chapter 8
News from Ticonderoga

Josiah Bradbury's Inn, a log house one and one half stories high, was one of the largest buildings in town. It faced Middle Street, conveniently close to the harbor for visiting mariners, and was distinguished not only for its size, but also for its sixteen sash windows filled with panes of glass. Glass was costly; panes had to be imported from Europe, or at least brought from Boston, packed carefully in crates of sawdust. Most houses, even those built of brick or wood planks and shingles, shuttered their windows against the cold and rains. Few had the luxury of allowing in light during inclement weather.

Rory looked at the inn in admiration. Inn-keeping must be a good business, indeed.

He followed Jonathan through the wide front door, his nose twitching. His stomach felt hollow as a drum, and the smells coming from inside were tempting.

Jonathan ordered oyster stew for each of them. Oysters were common this far up the Sheepscot, but not in Townsend Harbor, and Rory found them a welcome change from clams. He savored every bite, as he watched the other men and boys in the tavern and gulped his cider. Most talk at nearby tables was about the newly arrived vessels, and where they would be anchored, and for how long. Jonathan said little, motioning that they should listen, but not be obvious about it.

Rory was content to concentrate on his bowl and mug. The day had been long, and there was the excitement of a clandestine meeting yet to come.

As soon as they'd finished their meals he followed Jonathan out the back door into the fragrant kitchen garden where a group of nine young men had already gathered.

Most were dressed as Rory and Jonathan were, in worn breeches and long shirts. Their hair was of varied colors, but all wore it below their shoulders, pulled back and tied in a "tail" with a ribbon or thread at their necks.

Only one man wore long pants and a short jacket. His skin was darkened by sun and wind, and his hair, longer than that of the others, was braided in an untidy queue and tied with an eel skin. Clearly he was a mariner.

Rory nodded to those he'd seen on Fore Street that afternoon.

The boys seemed to have been waiting for Jonathan.

"You're finally here," said the one Rory remembered was called Ben. "We've been waiting for some minutes."

"I was supping inside," said Jonathan. "I've brought a new recruit. Meet Rory Campbell, from down to Boothbay. He knows what we're about, and he's game to join us."

Several of them nodded, but no one volunteered to introduce themselves.

"Who are you?" Jonathan asked, looking at the fellow with the queue.

"Dan Soule," he answered, stepping toward Jonathan. "Off the *Gruel*, just arrived, with a request from Captain White of the *Martha*."

outside, when no one else was nearby.

But who would she share thoughts with in Wiscasset? Rory and Mother would be in Boothbay. Sarah felt a shadow of loneliness pass through her, like a cloud moving in front of the sun.

"Sarah!" Mrs. Biddle called. "Your brother is here! Rory, have you found yourself something for supper?"

She joined them in the kitchen. Rory was being polite to Mrs. Biddle, but Sarah could tell by the way he glanced in her direction that he had something important to tell her.

"Aye, Ma'am. I had supper at Bradbury's Inn with Jonathan Decker."

Mrs. Biddle sniffed a bit. "I've heard that place is full of ideas to fill the brain as well as food to fill the stomach. If they asked me, I'd say men should get back to tending to their businesses and families instead of always talking about this war they've gotten themselves into. It would be better for all of us if everyone just shook hands and went home. Life could go back to the way it was before this nonsense changed the way people thought of themselves." She shook her head. "In any case, I'd guess you'll be needing a place to stay for the night, young man."

"If it wouldn't be a trouble."

"You can sleep on a pallet here in the kitchen, near your sister."

"Thank you, Ma'am."

They were silent for a few moments. Mrs. Biddle looked from Sarah to Rory and back again. "I expect you two will have thoughts to share before Rory leaves tomorrow, so I'll be off to my sleep. Sarah, you know where everything is. Leave the shutters and back door open to catch any breezes. This heat is tedious." She fanned herself with her hand and turned toward the door.

"Thank you, Mrs. Biddle," Sarah said.

"I'll see you in the morning, then," Mrs. Biddle replied. "It's nice having young people in the house. Don't you two worry about disturbing me if you want to talk a bit. I know you won't be seeing each other for a while. Once I get myself to bed I sleep as heavy as a brick bat. Nothing will wake me 'til the sun rises over the Sheepscot in the morning. Then I'll be up with the birds. Noisy creatures, those birds. Birds in England are much quieter."

Rory and Sarah listened to Mrs. Biddle's footsteps as she went to her bedchamber on the other side of the front hallway.

"Let me show ye my chamber," said Sarah, opening the door to her tiny space. "I have one all to myself."

Rory looked in. "Yer settled then, for now. Will ye be all right with Mrs. Biddle?"

Sarah held a finger to her lips and gestured for Rory to follow her out the back kitchen door. Mrs. Biddle, or perhaps someone acting at her direction, had planted what must have been intended to be a kitchen garden. Now there was just a mass of tall grasses and weeds, with a path worn through them to the privy.

"Mrs. Biddle says she sleeps heavy, but I don't know. The shutters are still open, so talk quietly," she whispered, sitting on a plank bench in the corner of the yard.

"Right ye are," Rory agreed, whispering. "In town I heard Mrs. Biddle's cousin the minister is a Tory. So look sharp! We don't want her learning any of our secrets and passing them on to British soldiers."

"It was not war secrets I was thinking of," said Sarah. "Not that we know any! I just thought we ought to have some privacy. Mrs. Biddle thinks the war is foolish, and would like to return to England, but I don't believe she'd do anything to sabotage the American Army. What could she do, even if she'd want to? We're in Wiscasset, Rory. Not Ticonderoga."

"So we are. But I've heard more goes on in Wiscasset than went on in Boothbay." Rory nodded sagely. "If you hear any secrets, Colonel Jones heads the Wiscasset militia. He's the one to tell."

"I'll remember. But I don't think Mrs. Biddle has any secrets the militia will be interested in."

Rory stood up. "Stop smiling at me as though I were a fool. I have something serious to tell you. And it does concern the war."

"Did anything happen to the gunpowder? It did get to the militia, didn't it?"

"So far as I know. That's not what I have to tell you." He paused. "I'm not going back to Boothbay with Jonathan tomorrow."

"What!" Sarah looked up at him. "You're going to stay in Wiscasset? Mother will be worried and Uncle angry, for sure, Rory."

Rory gave a halfway grin. "I'll send a message home with Jonathan. And they'll be more than worried and angry, Sarah. They'll be furious. Because I'm not staying in Wiscasset, either."

"Rory Campbell, what is it ye've dreamed up?" Sarah looked very stern. Rory had often done what was on his mind, not what he'd been told.

"Remember the *Martha*, the smaller vessel we saw in the harbor this afternoon? I'm going to help sail her back to Falmouth, and then I'm going to enlist in the York County militia." Rory spoke quickly, and didn't look directly at Sarah.

"Rory, no! Yer not sixteen, and ye've been told not to!"

"A man named Dan Soule says the Army at Ticonderoga – where Malcolm is! – needs more men, and they're calling for militia units to go. It's only for three months, and they're not particular about how old men are. Ye know we've heard before that not every regiment pays attention to the rules."

"But Mother, and Uncle ..."

"Mother and Uncle won't be there to stop me. Sarah, I'm old enough to decide for myself. I'm not needed in Boothbay. Hugh is

---

there for Mother and Uncle Andra and the Seacoast Defense, and you're here with Mrs. Biddle. Malcolm's in the Army. He and the other regulars need help. I'm *going* to volunteer for the militia. It's what I want to do."

"But ye have no gun, or even good boots. And what if ye should get hurt?" Sarah looked at Rory. "Or worse? I don't know if Mother could take it if she lost you, too."

"The fire that killed Father and Johnnie was over four years ago. They're gone. We can't spend our lives mourning. We're in a new land. We have new lives. And Mother has Uncle Andra now."

"Yer being hard and unfeeling!"

"I'm being a man, Sarah. I'm tired of being a boy who does everything he's supposed to. Others my age are fighting. I'll ask Jonathan to explain to Mother and Uncle I've gone to meet up with Malcolm; perhaps that will make them feel better. But I'm going, Sarah. I've decided."

They sat for a few minutes in silence. The night was hot, and the yard was dark. Only a little light from the half moon gave some contrast and shadows to the yard. Lightning bugs and mosquitos dodged here and there throughout the garden.

"I'm scared for ye, Rory. Scared ye'll be hurt."

"I'm scared too, Sarah. More than ye know. But I have to go. You have to understand." Rory paused. "It's one of the reasons I have to go. Because I'm so scared."

"What about your nightmares?"

"I lived when Johnnie died. I have to prove there was a reason for that, Sarah."

Sarah nodded, although in the dark Rory couldn't see her.

He couldn't see her tears, either.

And she couldn't see his.

Chapter 10
Jonathan's Challenge

Rory's dreams that night were, as always, filled with smoke and flames and screams. He forced himself to wake often, so he wouldn't moan or scream in his sleep and wake Sarah, as he often did. He would have to learn to control his nights, as he controlled his days. A soldier couldn't be scared by nightmares.

He lay awake in the dark, waiting for dawn, so he wouldn't have to fight the visions any longer.

He left Mrs. Biddle's home shortly after sunrise, before either she or Sarah had risen. He couldn't sleep, and he wanted to avoid saying goodbye to Sarah again, or having to explain anything to Mrs. Biddle.

Mariners were also up with the sun, and the *Martha* was being scrubbed down and polished in advance of her journey. Rory saw Dan on the dock, and raised his hand in greeting.

"You came," Dan said. "Did your family give you any arguments?"

"I have a cousin in the 11th Massachusetts, at Ticonderoga," said Rory, sidestepping the answer. "In Colonel Francis' regiment. We're not from Wiscasset; we're from Boothbay."

Dan nodded at him, and winked. "Not telling them now is your business. But you should send word. What's your name?"

"Rory Campbell. And I did tell my sister, who's staying here for the summer. Jonathan Brewer is heading for Boothbay later today, He'll take word to the rest of my family. I'm going to find him now. First I wanted ye to know I'd decided to go with ye."

"I'll look for you later this morning, Rory. Welcome to the *Martha*."

He found Jonathan at his skiff, loading mail and supplies ordered by those down river.

"I was about to knock on Mrs. Biddle's door to check on you," said Jonathan. "Tide's high in a couple of hours. I'd like to leave as soon as it turns, so we have the waters with us as we head for the ocean."

"I came to say I'm not going back with ye," Rory blurted.

"What?" Jonathan straightened up and looked at him.

"I'm sailing on the *Martha*. I've already talked to Dan."

"Your uncle will kill me if I don't bring you home. I don't care what Dan said last night. You're still young, Rory, and your family doesn't want you to join up. Continental Army or militia; they won't see the difference."

"I've made up my mind. My cousin Malcolm is at Ticonderoga. They need help there. Ye heard last night. I'm going."

"What use would you be to the militia? You've got no weapon or supplies. You've nothing but a boy's dreams of glory." Jonathan turned back to the skiff. "I won't help you, Rory. Wait a year or two. Wait until you're a man."

"In a year the war will be over, and I'll have missed my chance!" Rory pulled Jonathan's arm around until they were facing each other. "Explain to Uncle and Mother what I'm doing. Tell them ye tried to talk me out of it, but it was no use. I was too stubborn."

"I promised your family I'd bring you back to Boothbay, and that's what I'm doing, whether you like it or not!" Jonathan cocked his right arm and his fist moved fast, grazing Rory's chin as he ducked to the left.

Rory aimed a blow at Jonathan's nose in response, and blood spurted all over Jonathan's shirt.

Jonathan's left hand knocked Rory to the ground, where his head hit a rock. Rory shook his head and tried to stand up, but the world was going around too fast.

Jonathan grabbed a length of rope from the skiff and quickly tied Rory's hands in back of him, and then tied his feet together with the same length of rope.

The boys struggled with each other, but Jonathan was bigger and stronger. He hoisted Rory into the skiff and managed to get him onto the floor.

"Snake! Traitor! I thought ye were a friend! Yer just a . . ."

Jonathan ended Rory's howls by tearing a piece off the bottom of his long shirt and shoving it into Rory's mouth. "See if that quiets you down. No one can see you on the bottom of the skiff, and we'll be leaving in a couple of hours. When I promised to take you home, I meant it, even if I have to knock you out to do it! I have a few more deliveries to pick up before we leave. Stay quiet!"

Jonathan stomped up the low hill to the town, wiping his bloody nose with his shirt.

Rory twisted and turned. His head hurt. His back cramped where it lay against the planked floor of the boat. No one was near to see him or hear him.

Worst of all, if he didn't get loose he'd miss the *Martha*'s sailing.

Chapter 11
Sarah's Rescue

"Your brother must have been anxious to get off this morning," said Mrs. Biddle, as Sarah brought a pitcher of water in from the pump outside.

"He was gone when I woke," Sarah agreed. She'd been disappointed that he'd left without saying goodbye, but she'd already folded and replaced the quilt he'd slept on and swept off the pine kitchen floor.

"Young men are always in a hurry to get off to wherever they're not," said Mrs. Biddle. "When my husband and I were first married it seemed exciting that I never knew where he'd get himself to next, but after a few years it grew wearisome. I like to know when a person's going to be about, and when they're not. It helps considerable to be able to plans meals and such." She sighed. "But I suspect you know all about that, Sarah, living with a brother and two male cousins."

"Aye, yes, Mrs. Biddle," said Sarah, pouring water into the kettle they'd used for tea the day before.

"I'm sorry to see that young man rush off, though. I was going to give him the rest of the scones I baked yesterday, to take to your mother. Flour's dear these days, and I thought she might enjoy a taste of home, to thank her for sharing her daughter with an old woman this summer. Do you think he and that Jonathan have already left for Boothbay?"

"They were going to leave on the tide," said Sarah.

"Well, then, you're young and quick. Try and find them. Take the scones. They're in that tin box." Mrs. Biddle pointed at the first shelf of the yellow cupboard. "There's a muslin cloth in the drawer you can tie them up in."

Sarah followed her instructions.

"When you find that brother of yours, tell him next time he's visiting someone it's proper manners to stay to say his 'thank yous' for their hospitality, and not go running off at the crack of dawn when everyone is still abed."

"Aye, Mrs. Biddle," Sarah said, tightening the knot on the package of scones. "And I'm sure my mother will be much pleased to have these scones. I'll run quickly to be sure I find Rory before he and Jonathan cast off."

"Don't run so quickly it's improper, Sarah. You're a young lady under my care. I don't want you bringing shame to my household." Mrs. Biddle looked at her closely. "You're sure you know where they left their vessel?"

"Aye, Mrs. Biddle. I was on it just yesterday."

"Of course you were, dear, of course. Well, off with you, and come back when you've seen them safely gone."

"Aye, Mrs. Biddle."

Sarah closed the door as quickly as possible. One more chance to see Rory! Although he wouldn't be at the little skiff they'd come on yesterday; he'd be down on the sloop *Martha*.

In case Mrs. Biddle was watching, Sarah first turned toward where the skiff was tied, and then cut through an alleyway down toward the long wharves on the Sheepscot.

Mrs. Biddle was certainly a Tory; she didn't need to know Rory was sailing on the *Martha*. Or even that the *Martha* was sailing at all.

Men and boys crowded on the wharf, some just looking at the sloop as her crew prepared to sail, others busy loading barrels and wood shingles on board, headed for Falmouth.

Where was Rory? Sarah wished she knew someone in Wiscasset. She felt shy among all the strange men. Finally she found the courage to take a deep breath and ask an older man who seemed to be in charge of those loading barrels. "Please, is there a man by the name of Dan on the *Martha*?"

"Hey, DAN! Here's a pretty young lady to see you!" yelled the man.

Sarah's cheeks turned crimson, and others on the wharf turned and grinned at her. Some laughed.

A tall young man, perhaps as old as Malcolm, stepped off the sloop. "Looking for me, miss?" he asked.

"I'm trying to find my brother, Rory. He told me he was sailing with you today."

"Would your Rory be from Boothbay, and you the sister staying in Wiscasset?" asked Dan.

"Aye. Yes. I'm Sarah."

"Rory was here, sure enough, but some time ago. He said he was sailing with us, but left to see Jonathan, to send a message to his family. Haven't seen him since. Perhaps he changed his mind. We sail in half an hour. If you see him, tell him to get back here on the double, or he'll not be going with us."

"I will, sir. He did plan to sail with you. I'll try to find him."

"You do that. And I'm not a 'sir,' miss. I'm Dan. I hope your brother comes back. He seems a sharp fellow."

"He is, sir. And wants very much to go. I'll look for him now," Sarah said, as she turned and, forgetting Mrs. Biddle's reminder to act properly, ran the whole way down the wharf, dodging between people and boxes of cargo, headed for where Jonathan had tied the skiff the day before.

Where was Rory?

Chapter 12
The *Martha* Sails

Rory continued struggling against the ropes binding him. The heat was almost suffocating behind the shirt covering his mouth and part of his nose, and his wrists were now almost as sore and bleeding as his palms were from rowing so many hours the day before. He managed to kick off one of his low boots, but Jonathan had fastened the knots well. The ropes tightened instead of loosening.

Jonathan had returned twice to leave small bundles headed for Boothbay. "Don't fight so hard, Rory," he said once, sympathetically. "Understand I have to get you home. I promised your mother and uncle. They trusted me. As soon as we get clear of Wiscasset and the *Martha* has sailed I'll free you."

Rory's only answer had been to kick the side of the skiff as hard as he could.

Sarah ran the length of Water Street, where the long wharves were, and then turned, past the empty ship yards, to where Jonathan had tied the skiff.

Could Rory have changed his mind and decided not to sail on the Martha? But if that were so she was sure he would have come to tell her. He knew she was worried about his going to war. Right now she was worried about his disappearing.

The skiff was just where they'd left it yesterday, tied to a tree above the high tide mark. Now the incoming waters were only a few feet away; Jonathan would be leaving soon. Sarah slowed down. A few boxes were by the tree, but neither Rory nor Jonathan were nearby.

She walked slower, catching her breath as she approached the boat. The scones were still in her hand; she had tied them well. How could she explain to Mrs. Biddle that she was coming back with the scones because she couldn't find her brother?

She stood for a moment, thinking.

Then she heard a noise. A rough tapping, as though someone were knocking on a door. She listened again.

Slowly she walked toward the skiff. The noise got louder.

And then she saw.

"Rory! No! How did you get …?" Sarah ran the last couple of feet and reached down to help him. First she tore the cloth from his mouth. "What happened? No – don't answer. Turn, so I can get these knots undone." She helped Rory turn over and started working at the rope binding him.

"It was Jonathan! I told him what I was going to do, and asked him to tell Mother and Uncle, and he refused. He said he'd promised to take me home, and he'd take me back no matter what."

"Your wrists are bleeding!" Sarah said, as she finally freed Rory's wrists, and they both started working on the knots that held his ankles.

"How did you find me? What are you doing here?"

"Mrs. Biddle wanted to send some scones to Mother, so I went to find ye. I went to the *Martha*, and talked to that Dan ye told me about. He said ye'd be with Jonathan, so I came here."

"What time is it? I have to get to the *Martha*! Have they sailed?"

"Not yet. But Dan said you have to get there quickly. There!" The last of the rope came off.

Rory stood, unsteadily.

"Are you going to be all right?" asked Sarah. "Can you walk?"

"I'm going to be fine," said Rory. "My legs are just cramped. But I have to get to that sloop."

"Then I'm going with ye," said Sarah firmly. She put her arm around Rory's waist to steady him.

Glancing over their shoulders to make sure Jonathan wasn't returning to the skiff they half walked and half ran as quickly as they could back to where the *Martha* was anchored.

Dan waved to them as they approached the vessel. As they got closer, he saw the bruising and blood on Rory's wrists and ankles. "What happened to you, lad?"

"Someone tried to convince me I shouldn't go and enlist," said Rory.

Dan grimaced and shook his head. "Put some salt water on those sores before we sail, and you'll begin healing before we get to Falmouth. Your brother's a stubborn one, Sarah."

"Indeed he is," said Sarah, handing Rory the scones. "The British had better watch out when he's on the battle lines."

Rory grinned at her and gave her an awkward hug. "Thanks, Sarah. Write if ye find a way to get a letter through. I'll be with the York Militia, heading for Ticonderoga."

"Take care. And don't worry about Mother and Uncle. They'll accept what needs accepting."

Rory nodded.

"Come on, boy. Ship's a-sailin'. Time to meet your companions. You're not the only Wiscasset man to accept my invitation," said Dan, as Rory followed him on board the *Martha*, bound for Falmouth.

Chapter 13
Mrs. Biddle's Garden

"That took you long enough," said Mrs. Biddle as Sarah opened the door.

"I waited for them to leave," Sarah said, not mentioning which vessel it was that Rory had been on, or exactly why her errand had taken so long. "I wanted to wave farewell."

"Well, of course, it's your first time away from family, isn't it, dear?" Mrs. Biddle asked.

Sarah nodded.

"I remember my first time away from home. It was when Mr. Biddle and I were first married. Our families had known each other for years, of course, and we'd had a proper engagement of two years, but we'd never been alone, except in the drawing room on nights when my father fell asleep early." Mrs. Biddle smiled at the memory and even giggled a bit. "But we took a wedding journey to the sea. Fancy. I'd never seen the sea, and now I've sailed to the other side of it! But Mr. Biddle believed it would be an adventure for us. Instead I spent my first week as a married woman sobbing because I missed my mother and my dear home. Can you imagine, dear?"

Sarah missed her family, too, but, no, she couldn't imagine crying throughout her first week of married life. What must Mr. Biddle have thought?

"So if you get lonely for your home, or a bit teary, don't think I won't understand, because I will, my dear."

"Is there anything I can do for you this afternoon?" asked Sarah. Talking about crying was not making it any easier to think of Mother, twelve miles away downriver in Boothbay, and Rory, on his way to an unknown future on the *Martha*.

"The garden needs tending, dear. If you could do that it would be a great solace to me. The drought has been very hard on it. My dear cousin was able to get some seeds for me, and a young lady who lives nearby and her brother were kind enough to dig a space and plant them for me, but I'm afraid I can't do much weeding at my age." Mrs. Biddle shook her head. "It's all gotten quite beyond me, I'm afraid."

Sarah looked out the kitchen door into the yard. What Mrs. Biddle must be calling the garden looked like a tangle of dried weeds. "I know little about gardens. Mother is trying to grow beans and corn, but the ground in Boothbay is too rocky and dry. We had a few flowers in Falkirk, but that was all."

"It can't be that difficult. People here seem to manage," said Mrs. Biddle, coming to stand by Sarah at the door.

"What is planted there?" Sarah asked.

"I wanted flowers. Roses and lilies and jonquils and daisies to remind me of home. But food supplies are uncertain in these times, and one must do what is necessary." Mrs. Biddle sighed deeply. "I believe they planted squash and pumpkins and cabbage. And parsnips. Dreadful vegetables, actually, but they store well, my cousin said, and Americans seems to relish them. And beans, I think he said. There was no space for corn."

They both stood and looked at the large plot filled with thriving weeds.

"Perhaps if you talked with the young lady who planted the seeds, she would know what to do," said Mrs. Biddle. "That would be just the idea! I once asked if she could come by, but she was busy caring for her younger brothers and sisters. Her mother does keep having children. And one or more of her brothers have enlisted, I believe. But perhaps she could explain to you what must be done."

"I could ask," said Sarah, doubtfully. The garden looked beyond hope.

Mrs. Biddle nodded. "You go on over and ask. Her name is Betsey Parsons, and she lives in the red house behind ours, on Fort Hill Street. You won't be able to miss it. It's across from that dreadful log building that blocks our view of the river."

"What is that building?" asked Sarah.

"The Bradbury Inn. Mr. Josiah Bradbury, who runs it, is no better than the mariners and revolutionaries who drink their rum and cider there," said Mrs. Biddle. "And noise! If I weren't a God-fearing woman I'd be saying something dreadful about the fearsome racket that comes out of the windows and doors of that place! Mr. Biddle and I would never have selected this location for a house, but, of course, it was my dear cousin, the Reverend Bailey, who made the choice, and I am certain he could not have dreamed of the riotous doings that occur so close by." Mrs. Biddle shook her head. "If you hear anything that begins to sound inappropriate for a decent girl's ears, you just close the shutters in your chamber, and sing hymns, Sarah. That's what I advise. That's what I do myself."

Chapter 14
The *Martha* at Sea

Dan introduced Rory to Captain White, a wide, bearded man, his skin red with sun and wind. Seeing the condition of Rory's blistered hands and torn wrists and ankles, he shook his head. "Lucky we found three new men to crew out of Wiscasset. You won't be much good to me or to the militia until those hands are healed."

"I can work, Captain. My hands won't be a problem."

Captain White clapped Rory on the shoulder. "You're eager to be of service, and a man eager to labor should do so. If I need you to haul ropes, I'll call, but for now I'm putting you on lookout for Admiral Collier's vessels, or any other enemy forces."

"Yes, sir," said Rory.

"If you see any vessels, come to me directly and quietly so I can check its flag and markings with my glass," said Captain White. "Be certain not to alarm the crew. In these days ships can all too easily be taken for what they are not – on either side. It's best I make the call."

"Yes, sir."

"To your position on the prow, then!" said Captain White.

Rory stood, braced against the railing at the front of the *Martha*, carefully watching both the shoreline and horizon. The chance of Admiral Collier's vessels, or any other British ships, being in the

Sheepscot River this afternoon were slight, but he stood tall, focusing on the horizon. He was entrusted with responsibility for the *Martha* and its crew.

When they left Southport Island behind and turned south, away from Townsend Harbor and Boothbay and into the Atlantic Ocean, he took a deep breath. His new life was beginning. Now there was no turning back, even if he had wished to do so.

As they passed the entrance to the Kennebec River, Dan and two other men approached him. "Rory! Do you know the others who joined us in Wiscasset?"

One of the men Rory thought he recognized from the group at Bradbury's Inn; the other he didn't know.

"Meet Ethan Chase and Sam Riggs. Men, this is Rory Campbell, out of Boothbay. He aims to enlist, too."

"Pleased to meet you." Rory ignored his painful palm and wrist and firmly shook their hands. Ethan didn't look much older than he was, but was taller, his hair wavier and darker brown, and his lightly pox-marked face showed he'd had the smallpox.

Sam was perhaps in his mid-twenties, and dressed in better clothing than either Rory or Ethan. He was also more equipped for war; a cartridge pouch and a hunting knife hung from his belt, and his boots weren't worn, as were those of most Maine men in these times.

"Are ye both from Wiscasset?" asked Rory.

"I am," said Ethan. "Been wanting to enlist, and finally got Ma to agree."

Perhaps he was the one who'd said he was going to check with his mother before coming with Dan. Rory wondered if his own mother knew yet that her son had headed south, and wasn't coming back to Boothbay. Not for months. He tried not to think of her, and focused on the men with him.

"I'm from Damariscotta," answered Sam. "Happenstance I was in Wiscasset and heard Captain White needed crew. Thought I'd take the opportunity."

"You've been on watch for a time, Rory," said Dan. "Captain White's sending another man to take your place. Cook's got supper ready."

Rory had put his scones below deck, but knew he didn't have enough for all, so didn't mention them. He'd savor them later.

The three men headed back to the small shed on deck that served for cooking, and they each took a plate of warmed-over corn and bean stew. It wasn't tasty, but it was filling.

"So you're for the York militia, too?" Rory asked Ethan.

"For sure," said Ethan, his eyes shining. "If there were another Lincoln County regiment forming, that would be the one. But since there isn't, York sounds good to me." He took off his brown felt hat and pointed at the inside, where a spruce twig was drawn.

"Why is there a picture in yer hat?" asked Rory.

"For the District of Maine!" said Ethan. "I heared you could tell a District of Maine man in the war by the spruce twig he wore in his hat. That didn't make no sense to me, since a twig would brown and fall off before a man'd get south of New Hampshire. But I'm a Maine man, no doubt, so I found me a way to take a spruce twig that won't die or be lost."

"Aye! That's smart," said Rory, admiring the drawing. "Did ye do it yer own self?"

"I'm not real good with words, but I can do pictures," nodded Ethan. "It's rough, but you can tell it's a spruce twig, right enough."

"Yer an artist, no doubt! Will ye draw a spruce twig inside my hat, too, before we get to Falmouth? I like yer idea of carrying a bit of Maine with me."

"If we can find some charcoal, I could," said Ethan. "The cook might have some. In York there'll be a fire, for sure. I could do it there. I've heard after you sign up you do a lot of waiting."

"Then we'll have something to pass the time," said Rory. "I'll hold ye to it."

While they were talking, Sam had disappeared below decks.

"Guess Sam is checking on our supplies," said Ethan. "He helped load everything on board in Wiscasset. I thought he was working for the lumberyard, he was moving so many barrels."

"What're in the barrels on board?" asked Rory, as Dan joined them.

"Most were made at the lumberyard in Wiscasset, going to Falmouth to be used there. Two small ones are filled with gunpowder made by folks in this area of the coast for use by our army and militia. And two or three are filled with household goods going to the daughter of someone in Wiscasset who married a Falmouth man a month or two back. Just the usual supplies to be shipped."

"How long will it take for us to reach Falmouth?" asked Rory. "The sun is about to set." The sun was already low; red and orange streaks ran through the dark waters on the horizon. The sky was black but for a lacework of stars and the half moon that lit part of the deck and left the rest in shadows.

"We're passing the mouth of the New Meadows River now. We'll sail slowly, with no light but the moon. No ships should see us as we enter Casco Bay. We must also be still. Noise travels too well over water."

"But," Ethan interrupted, "We won't be able to see the British ships either, in the dark!"

Dan nodded. "Therein's the danger. Captain White knows these waters well. He'll keep us from hitting the ledges and islands throughout the Bay. But some islands are large enough to conceal a ship during the night, and we won't know where they are until daybreak. That's the most dangerous time for us. When daylight breaks we don't know what we'll see. Or who will see us."

Ethan and Rory looked at each other.

"Sleep well, boys. It will be an early morning, and we'll need all hands on deck in case of trouble."

Chapter 15
Sarah Becomes a Spy

Sarah had already removed her apron and mob cap and put on her outdoor bonnet in preparation for leaving Mrs. Biddle's home for the second time that day. She'd determined to find Betsey Parsons and ask her about Mrs. Biddle's garden, when there was a knock on the front door.

The tall man standing there wore an elegant formal white wig tied with a black ribbon in a neat queue and a gray fitted coat, waistcoat, and breeches. He looked almost as surprised to see Sarah as she did to see him. In her entire year in Maine she had not seen anyone dressed as fashionably as this gentleman.

Mrs. Biddle pushed Sarah aside, and enveloped him in one of her enormous embraces. "Jacob, Jacob! Dear cousin! How wonderful to see you! It's been such a long time! Come in, come in, you must come in and sit down!"

She held on to his arm as she almost pulled him into the kitchen.

"It is most certainly good to see you, too, cousin," he said. "But have I interrupted you? You already have a guest." He nodded at Sarah, who backed up toward the corner of the small kitchen and curtsied slightly.

"This is Sarah Campbell, who journeyed with me last year. She lives in Boothbay, and has come to keep me company now that my dear Mr. Biddle has left this world." Mrs. Biddle pulled a handkerchief from her pocket and touched it to her eyes. "I miss him so, Jacob. My days are empty without him."

"Of course you miss him. That is one reason I've come to call; to see how you were faring. But now I know you are not alone, I will not be as concerned for you."

This man must be the Reverend Bailey. Mrs. Biddle had not mentioned any other cousins in Maine.

"Sarah, would you pour Jacob and me some tea, please?" asked Mrs. Biddle. "You know where everything is. And, Jacob, you must tell me everything. How have you been? Have you any news from our friends in England?"

Sarah put another log on the fire and checked to be certain there was water enough in the kettle for two cups of tea. That Mrs. Biddle had offered the Reverend a cup of tea was certainly proof of what Rory had said; the Reverend was a British sympathizer. Although, Sarah admitted silently, she herself had indulged in a cup just yesterday. Perhaps it was possible Mrs. Biddle's cousin drank tea as she had done, only to please the lady herself.

She put the teacups and teapot on the table and placed the tea caddy and two spoons next to it.

"I've heard little from England," Reverend Bailey was saying. "So far my fervent request for a new parish there or in Nova Scotia has been met with silence. Few ships are carrying messages, and I've waited in vain to hear an answer to my petition for a new ministerial post. Of course, I've asked that you should accompany me if I am reassigned to a parish in a more hospitable area."

"Let us hope you receive word soon. Did you walk the entire way from Pownalborough? You must be exhausted!" Mrs. Biddle said.

"I walked part of the way yesterday, and stayed the night with a parishioner before resuming my walk today," replied Reverend Bailey. "Of course, I was anxious to see you. And I always enjoy visiting this charming village. It is so different from where I live."

"How so?" asked Mrs. Biddle, carefully measuring out the tea.

"We who live near the Kennebec River seldom see vessels of any size in these difficult days. And yet I couldn't help but notice that this afternoon there is a large ship anchored here in your harbor."

"Is there? My dear, you know I seldom leave the house. The comings and goings of men and ships is of no interest to me."

"And certainly there is no reason for a lady like yourself to be concerned with such details," said the Reverend, reaching out and patting Mrs. Biddle's plump hand. "But I did stop at Whittier's Tavern to refresh myself, and there discovered some information of interest. A man of my acquaintance and sympathies told me the ship in the harbor – the *Gruel* it is called – a most unfortunate name – is here by order of the Continental Army, to be filled with masts for the French Navy."

"Is it now?" asked Mrs. Biddle, her eyes growing large. "But we English are not allowing such trade, are we?"

"Indeed we are trying to prevent it. I suspect it will be quite difficult for these small-town mariners to get that ship from Wiscasset to France without confronting one of his Majesty's ships. They're patrolling the seas of this northeast coast with some frequency. It is surprising the ship was able to arrive here without detection."

"I would think so," declared Mrs. Biddle.

No one paid attention to Sarah, who sat quietly in the corner. Rory was right. Reverend Bailey was certainly a Tory. And he was clearly not pleased at the *Gruel*'s being in Wiscasset. Did Reverend Bailey have ways to contact Admiral Collier and signal him that the *Gruel* was here? The ship would have to be loaded and leave Wiscasset as soon as possible if Captain Proctor were to avoid Admiral Collier.

Any Scots lass knew the French detested the English. They had a long history of wars with the English, and might well be persuaded to join this war on the side of the Americans. But first the Americans would have to prove their worth as a strong ally.

Those masts might help convince them to send ships and troops to help the American army. The *Gruel* and its cargo had to be kept safe.

Sarah sat very still. Who did she know in Wiscasset who could help? One girl, even one who was almost thirteen, couldn't stop the British Navy.

But maybe one girl could warn the local militia that Reverend Bailey knew about the *Gruel*, and that he planned to get word to the British that the vessel was in Wiscasset.

Chapter 16
Trouble on board the *Martha*

Rory began to realize how weary he was. Was it only two days ago that he and Sarah had set off with Jonathan from Boothbay? He climbed down into the hold of the *Martha*, hoping for a few hours sleep, and remembering the scones Mrs. Biddle had thought she was sending to Mother.

Mother would have enjoyed them. But not enough for him to have risked seeing Jonathan again after their fight on the waterfront. He settled into the corner where he'd tucked the scones. Where had Mrs. Biddle found raisins to add to them? He took small bites and savored each crumb.

A few minutes later Ethan joined him.

"It's dark as a grave down here," Ethan said. "Is that you, Rory?"

"Aye; it is. Are ye alone?"

"I am. I'm aiming at catching some sleep before they wake me for the next watch."

Rory reached out, and handed him a scone. "Here, then. My sister's staying with Mrs. Biddle for the summer, and she baked these. Do ye like scones?"

"Scones? Never heard of them." Ethan took a bite. "Where did she find flour and raisins? And sugar, I'll wager. I'll draw you a spruce *tree* for this!" He chewed quietly for a few moments. "We won't be getting food like this in the militia. Mrs. Biddle is the woman who came with her husband from England last summer, isn't she? The one who's related to Reverend Bailey over to Pownalborough?"

"Aye. She and her husband sailed on the same ship with my family. We were all held over in Nova Scotia until a vessel could be found that would take us to Maine. With times so uncertain it was difficult to find a vessel to sail into an American port."

"I thought you was talking different! You're from England?" Ethan scuttled backward a foot or so. "How do I know you're not a Tory, when we're sitting here eating Tory scones?"

"I'm not English. I'm a Scotsman. Or was until I came here, and became an American, same as ye. Scotsmen hate the English, same as Americans. Only difference is, in Scotland we've got to live in the country next to 'em and fight for 'em in their armies. Celebrate their holidays with 'em, too. They've got some good ones, I'll give 'em that. Like Guy Fawkes Day, when there's bonfires and fireworks."

"What's that to celebrate?"

"Couple of hundred years ago some fellows tried to blow up Parliament with gunpowder and got caught."

"Too bad they got caught. Maybe we should fill a vessel with gunpowder and try it again!" said Ethan.

"That's an idea!" Rory laughed. "When we see General Washington perhaps we should tell him about it!"

"You *are* one of us, then?" said Ethan.

"I'm no Tory, for sure. My cousin's with Colonel Francis at Ticonderoga, and I figure to join him there. Didn't Dan say that's where the militia's being called out to?"

"He did that," Ethan agreed. They were both silent for a few minutes. "You got any more of those scone things?"

"One for each of us, and that's the end," said Rory, handing one of the last two precious pastries to Ethan. "Now ye *do* owe me a spruce tree – or maybe two!"

They sat comfortably in the darkened hold, their backs against barrels. Once in a while they heard footsteps above them on the deck, or another man would climb down into the hold, or leave and head back up topside. It had been a long day, and the rolling and swaying of the ship made them drowsy.

Rory's dreams confused the moaning and creaking of the sloop with the cracking of the beams of his burning home; the roof beginning to give way. He sat up suddenly, shaking his head to rid himself of the visions and noises in his head. But the sounds didn't stop.

He focused his eyes in the dim light of the hold. Above him he could see the pale gray of first light between planks on the deck. He must have slept longer than he'd thought. He glanced next to him. Ethan wasn't there. But in the far corner of the hold, he could see the silhouette of a man using an iron bar to pry up the wooden head of one of the smaller barrels.

The creaking sound he'd heard was that of iron rubbing on wood.

Those smaller barrels held gunpowder.

The shadowy man removed the head, took something from under his coat, and filled it. He held it carefully, put the head back on the barrel, and headed toward the ladder to the deck.

No man would open a barrel of gunpowder on a ship unless a battle was raging. And that man had taken more gunpowder than would be needed to fill a powder horn.

The thief climbed toward the deck. New morning light was now on his face, and Rory recognized him. It was Sam, the volunteer from Damariscotta. And maybe he'd been talking too much about Guy Fawkes Night and Scotland, or dreaming about the fire. But he thought he recognized what Sam had hidden under his coat.

Quickly he followed Sam onto the deck.

"Good morning," he said, stretching, as though he'd just wakened.

Sam turned around, startled. "I didn't know anyone was below decks."

"Just woke. I'm a heavy sleeper. Where are we?"

"Casco Bay. Not far from Falmouth. We should be docking by mid-morning if winds stay steady." Sam started to walk toward the small wooden box, the caboose, containing the cook's stove.

Rory walked with him. He didn't dare leave Sam alone. If his guess was right, he had to stop Sam from what he was going to do. Sam was going to put everyone, and everything, on the *Martha* in danger.

"Beautiful day. Are ye going to enlist in the York Militia?" asked Rory. "I don't remember yer saying."

"I didn't say," said Sam. "Why don't you find your friend Ethan and see what he's doing?"

"He's probably busy," said Rory. "Have ye been to Falmouth before?"

"Once, before the British burned it two years ago. It was a handsome town then." Sam was standing next to the caboose.

Rory moved so his body blocked its door. The stove inside would contain heat, and perhaps fire. That's what Sam wanted. That's what Rory must keep him from getting. "They must be rebuilding the town, then. Or planning to do so after the war's been won. I'm looking forward to seeing it. I've heard it's one of the largest towns in Maine. Or was, before the fire."

The *Martha* was a small sloop. Other men were nearby. But if he was right, there wasn't time to get help. It would only take a moment for Sam to put them in danger.

If he were wrong, he would be a laughingstock. But if he were right, he might save the sloop from the British.

Dan was in the stern, talking to another crew member.

"Look!" he pointed. "There's Dan!"

Sam glanced toward the stern of the boat.

In that instant, Rory dove at him, grabbing both his knees, and knocking him to the deck of the *Martha*. "Dan!" he yelled. "Help!"

Dan was there in three steps. "What are you doing?"

Rory was on the deck, clinging to Sam's legs. Sam struggled to get up.

Gunpowder was spilling from the inside of Sam's coat onto both the men and the deck.

"Help me!" gasped Rory. "He's trying to alert the British to where we are!"

"This boy is a lunatic! Get him off me!" yelled Sam. "He doesn't know what he's talking about!"

By then most of the crew had gathered around them. Two men pulled Rory off Sam, and another two held Sam. The two glared at each other.

Captain White took charge. "What is this all about? Sam, you first."

"I was standing here, enjoying the fresh sea air, when this insane young man grabbed my legs and started screaming and pulling me down. Thank goodness you were all here to ensure that he didn't push me overboard!"

"What have you to say, Rory?"

"I saw Sam opening one of the barrels of gunpowder in the hold. He poured the powder into a piece of rolled paper. Ye'll find the paper in his inside coat pocket, and I think ye'll find a tightly rolled paper soaked with saltpeter at the bottom of the rolled paper."

Several of the men started murmuring.

Captain White looked at Sam. Then he reached over and opened

Sam's jacket. The inside was now streaked with gunpowder, but, just as Rory had said, the two connected rolls of paper were there in Sam's coat pocket.

"Rory's correct! This is a crude firework! You were going to light the saltpeter fuse to send up a gunpowder rocket. That would have alerted any British ships in the area to our presence!" Captain White's accusation was firm.

"My loyalty is to the Crown!" Sam shouted.

"Tie him up. We'll turn him over to the authorities in Falmouth. And clean this loose gunpowder off the deck near the cook's caboose immediately, before any of it ignites!" Captain White turned to Rory. "How did you recognize the rocket?"

"The father of a friend of mine in Scotland set off fireworks on Guy Fawkes Day, sir. Sometimes he let me help. His were a lot larger, of course."

Captain White clapped him on the shoulder. "I thank you for keeping your wits about you. You'll make a fine member of the York militia, Rory Campbell."

"Thank you, sir." Rory grinned.

"And now, everyone, settle down! We should be safely in Falmouth within the hour!"

Chapter 17
Sarah and Colonel Jones

Reverend Bailey stayed for supper, and it wasn't until Mrs. Biddle's nap the next afternoon that Sarah was able to get away. "To meet Betsey Parsons, and ask her about your garden," she explained, as Mrs. Biddle nodded drowsily in agreement.

Rory had said Colonel Jones was the head of the Wiscasset militia. He was the one who must be told about Reverend Bailey's knowledge of the *Gruel*. Rowdy men with wild ideas were at Bradbury's Inn, and that's where Rory and Jonathan had dined. Certainly one of those men would know where she could find Colonel Jones.

She stood outside the door of the inn for a few minutes. Despite the heat of the day her hands were icy cold. What had made her think someone as important as a colonel of the militia would listen to a twelve-year-old girl? But she had to try. This was important information. It must get to someone who could act on it.

Despite its windows, the large front room of the inn was low and dark even in the middle of the day and stank of sweaty men and spirits and tobacco. Sarah tried not to gag. As she stood in the doorway everyone turned to look at her, and she realized she was the only female in the room. Then an old man came out from the kitchen. "How may I help you?" he asked, looking at her curiously.

"I'm looking fer Colonel Jones, of the Wiscasset Militia," Sarah said, very quietly. Everyone in the room was listening.

"It's him in the green shirt over there by the window," said the man, pointing at a heavyset man in the corner. He shook his head at Sarah, and returned to the kitchen.

"Thank you kindly," said Sarah. She wished she could turn around and run. But doing that would make these old men laugh. That would be worse than having them stare at her as though she were a unicorn in a pigpen. She walked with determination over to the man in the green shirt.

"Would ye be Colonel Jones?" she asked.

"I am. Who's asking?"

"Sarah Campbell, from Boothbay. I am currently staying with Mrs. Biddle, over on Fort Hill Street."

"So you're a Tory, are you? And you want to talk with me?" Colonel Jones spit on the ground, next to Sarah's feet. "That's what I think of Tories, girl, whatever you call yourself. Go home to Mrs. Biddle and pray for your king. He's going to need all the prayers he can get when we're through with his army!"

The men all broke into hearty laughter.

Sarah moved back a bit, but stood her ground. "I'm not a Tory. My cousin's in the 11th Massachusetts, and my brother's left on the *Martha* to enlist in the York County Militia to help at Ticonderoga." She looked around the room. All the men were watching her, grinning as though she were an entertainment at a carnival. She was doing the right thing. Why wouldn't they take her seriously? She raised her voice and spoke to all of them. "Why aren't all ye brave patriots fighting for our independence in the Army instead of sitting here drinking rum?" She turned back to Colonel Jones. "Please. I need to speak with ye in private."

"She's a little young for you, Jones!" said the man sitting next to the Colonel.

"God gives and he takes, it's true," said Mrs. Parsons. "And sometimes," she looked around the room, "he gives a bit more than we plan for." She opened the back door. "Betsey! Get in here!"

"Coming, Ma!" The girl who almost ran into Mrs. Parsons was clearly Betsey. Her two braids might have begun the day pinned to the top of her head, because one, indeed, was still there under her mob cap. But the other flapped curiously loose around one ear. Her apron was askew, and she wasn't wearing shoes or stockings. "I heared you the first time you called!" She put down the large book she was carrying.

"This is Sarah Campbell from Boothbay, come to see you. She's staying with Mrs. Biddle."

"How do you do," said Sarah.

"Did Mrs. Biddle send you, then?" asked Betsey. "You're new to town!"

"I'm here to keep her company for a while. And she did send me. She told me you planted her garden. She'd like me to weed it fer her, and thought ye might tell me where it was ye planted what, so I'd know what to look fer under the grasses that've overgrown it."

Mrs. Parsons shook her head. "Why don't you girls go and take a little walk and talk about this garden of Mrs. Biddle's and get acquainted? T'would be good for you to get out of the privy, Betsey, and talk to someone your own age. I can manage here well enough for a while."

"Thank you, Ma!" said Betsey. She headed for the door, pulling on her shoes at the same time.

"Wait! While you're walking, would you walk in the direction of the wharf and find your pa and tell him he's expected home for supper tonight? You tell him I said no excuses even if he should have to work late at the lumberyard again."

"Yes, Ma," said Betsey, grabbing Sarah's hand.

And they were out on Fort Hill Street.

Sarah looked at Betsey. "Are all those children your brothers and sisters?"

"Every one. My brother Ben is probably with Pa. There's eight of us now. Was ten, but one died real early, and the oldest of us, Adam, went with General Arnold to Quebec two years ago and wasn't one of those to come home. Joseph's with General Washington's Army. Don't you have a big family?"

"Not *that* big," said Sarah. "My brother Rory is fourteen, and after my father died my mother married my uncle, so my two cousins are sort of brothers now. But they're all grown up. They're twenty and twenty-two."

"That sounds complicated," said Betsey.

"Maybe complicated, but not as noisy," said Sarah. "Why do ye hide in the privy? Your mother said ye read in there!"

"It's the only quiet place! Sometimes I take our family Bible in there."

Sarah almost giggled. "You take the Bible into the privy? Do ye think the Lord would approve?"

"If he made us, he made our bodies, too!" Betsey replied. "Besides, it's the only book we have. And there are good stories in there." She paused. "How old are you?"

"Twelve. And you?"

Betsey stood tall. "I was twelve last month."

They were walking toward the river when Sarah stopped. "Yer mother said yer father would be on the wharf or at the lumberyard. Is he one of those preparing masts for the *Gruel*?"

"He's in charge of the whole job. He's the one ensuring that the masts and wood for the French are cut and loaded on the *Gruel* as soon as possible," Betsey said proudly. Then she confided, "The lumberyard hasn't had an order that large in more than a year, so no wood is waiting to be loaded. Pa's talked of nothing else in days. Ma's peeved 'cause he's been forgetting to do chores she asked him to finish."

"Betsey Parsons, does that means ye and yer family are all patriots, fer sure?" Sarah asked.

"Of course we are!" Betsey looked at Sarah as though she were daft. "I told you Adam died serving with General Arnold. Do we look like rich Tories or English folks? I should be asking YOU. You're the one living with Mrs. Biddle. Everyone knows *she's* a Tory."

"She is. But I'm not. I've a brother with the militia and a cousin who's a regular. Betsey, I need to talk with yer father about the *Gruel*. He needs to hide the ship if he's going to keep it away from the British! I know someone's who's going to get word to Admiral Collier that it's here in Wiscasset."

Betsey looked at Sarah. "How do you know that? Are you sure you're not a Tory?" Then she whispered, "Or maybe you're a spy?"

Sarah looked startled, and then they both started to giggle.

"I donna think so," said Sarah. "But maybe I could be! I do need to talk to yer father. It's important."

Betsy nodded. "I'll introduce you to him, as soon as we find him at the dock."

Sarah felt as though the clouds had just parted. She *would* be able to deliver the message that Reverend Bailey would tell the British about the *Gruel*. Someone could do something about it after all! "I'm glad Mrs. Biddle sent me to meet ye. And after we talk with your father, ye and I need to talk about gardens."

The two girls grinned at each other and headed down the hill toward the Sheepscot River, to where the *Gruel* was anchored.

SEPTEMBER, 1777

Chapter 20
Men of the Militia

By the time they reached Wells, where Lieutenant Colonel Joseph Storer was enlisting men, Rory and Ethan knew each other well.

They'd learned both of their fathers were dead, and, while Rory's mother had remarried, Ethan's had not, so he'd been relieved to know their enlistment was for only three months. "I'll be home before the new year," he confided to Rory. "Ma needs me to work our farm. But I wanted to be a part of making our nation free. Someday I want to be able to tell my grandchildren I did my part."

Grandchildren! That seemed a long time in the future. Right now Rory was just proud to be a private in Storer's Regiment: the 3rd York County Massachusetts Militia. Sometimes he repeated it over to himself just to hear the words. The regiment was fortunate in its officer: Joseph Storer was a fair man, well-liked by his men, and an experienced soldier.

Ethan was kept busy drawing charcoal spruce twigs and trees on the hats and shirts and wooden canteens of the men in the regiment. He even drew one on the outside of Colonel Storer's tent. "With your help, we'll all carry the District of Maine proudly into battle," said the Colonel, as he admired Ethan's work. "When this war is over, you should do something with that skill of yours, soldier. You have talent."

They waited in Wells, marching and drilling, much as Rory remembered seeing boys playing at doing on the Wiscasset Green. They cleaned their muskets and practiced loading them quickly, and aiming them – a man quick with his musket could shoot three or four times in a minute – but they didn't fire. Gunpowder was too scarce to waste on practice.

Crickets sang at night, and goldenrod bloomed yellow in the fields. Summer was coming to a close.

Some men had brought muskets and knives and heavy boots and powder horns with them. But Maine's isolated towns had suffered sorely during the years England's vessels controlled the seas. Rory and Ethan were not alone in having no blankets, coats, or extra clothing.

One town sent the militia a crate of boots, with a note saying men in Maine would sooner go barefoot than have their fighting men do the same.

Colonel Storer had a tent garnered from his days in the regular army, but his men slept on the ground, rain or shine. They were all grateful when one afternoon a wagon arrived filled with blankets collected by church women in Arundel. Ethan and Rory each received one. After that they had something more than homespun shirts between their skin and the cold ground at night.

Finally the new regiment started south. A week's marching took them to Cambridge, near Boston, where they met up with another newly formed militia regiment and four supply wagons. About two dozen wives of men in that unit came along, too, to wash and cook and nurse any men who should need it.

Together they walked west, across the farms and small towns of Massachusetts and over the Berkshire Mountains, toward the Hudson River. No one knew what was happening with the two armies opposing each other there. They just knew they needed to get there as soon as they could.

A few men became ill along the way and fell behind. More joined in. Some were boys as young as twelve; others, men in their sixties. Most were white, but there were black men, too, and Indians as well. Some women carried muskets as well as cooking pots.

The militia was no place for children. But a few children and more than a few dogs ran between the wheels of the wagons until the officers ordered that they be carried by the women, or left behind.

Most volunteers were farmers, walking past fields waiting to be harvested and hoping those left behind would be able to bring in their crops so their families would have food for the winter. Others were craftsmen: coopers, tanners, shoemakers, tailors, weavers; or fishermen, lumbermen, ship builders or mariners.

All had the words "liberty" and "freedom" on their lips and in their hearts.

Along the way they heard rumors that some Iroquois Indians were fighting on the British side. The Indians were said to travel ahead of the British troops. Their scouts knew the countryside and could creep through the forests and spy on the colonists without being seen or heard. They then told the British when and where to attack. But some of the Indians had also been said to scalp women and children, Tory and Patriot alike, in their beds. Some Tory families had turned Patriot because of it.

Other Indians, like the Pequots, had joined Patriot militia regiments in Connecticut and were heading for upstate New York.

Patriot forces near Bennington, Vermont British forces in a battle there. ("Vermont?" someone asked. "Isn't Vermont another country?" "So they say," was the reply. "What does it matter, long as whoever's there's on our side.")

As he walked, day after day, the soles of his feet hardened with walking, Rory thought of Malcolm. Had he survived the attack on Ticonderoga and the retreat? And he thought of home. Had Sarah stayed with Mrs. Biddle in Wiscasset? Were Mother and Uncle Andra and Hugh safe? Did they have enough to eat?

Leaves changed from green to yellow and red. Early morning fogs and frosts chilled the men sleeping on the cold ground. Rory shivered in his light shirt.

Whatever battle was to take place must be fought before winter snows set in. No army of thousands of men could survive heavy winter snows in the wilderness of northern New York State. There'd be no way to get them the supplies they'd need.

Colonel Storer pushed his men to walk faster, for more hours each day. By now many of the men had holes in shoes already well-worn when they'd joined the regiment. Rory's were barely holding together. He'd torn pieces off his shirt to line them, to help the leather last. Shirts, breeches, and waistcoats were now tattered. No one had stockings. Only hats, although worn and stained, were relatively undamaged. ("We don't walk on them. Not yet, anyway!" Ethan said cheerfully one afternoon, as he drew still another spruce twig on a hat that had somehow escaped his charcoal.)

But spirits remained high.

Their one fear was that the battle would be over before they arrived. That all their weeks of hunger and sore feet and wet clothes and nights on hard ground far from home would have been for nothing.

And there was one other fear few said aloud.

"Rory, are you afeared to die?" Ethan whispered one night as they lay on the ground, trying to sleep, their stomachs empty but for some walnuts they'd found on the ground that afternoon.

For a few moments Rory didn't reply. "I don't think I'm afraid of being dead. That means yer gone. Maybe to Heaven, or maybe someplace else. I don't know. But yer not here anymore. But – I'm afraid of the pain."

"I've thought of that, too. The pain. And watching other men die. And I keep wondering what it would be like to kill someone. To watch them die and know you took the life out of them." They were both quiet. "I don't know if I can do it."

"I don't know either," said Rory. "But I guess we'll be finding out soon enough."

"Maybe it would be better not to think on it," whispered Ethan.

"Perhaps," agreed Rory. "But it's a hard thing not to do."

Chapter 21
Sarah and Betsey on the Sheepscot

"Sarah Campbell, you're moving faster than a rabbit chased by a fox! I'm guessing you and Betsey Parsons have plans for this afternoon. Am I right?" Mrs. Biddle sat at her usual place by the front window in the kitchen, watching Sarah move quickly from one task to another.

Sarah nodded. "I've finished the weeding, the dishes are washed, and the house is swept. Betsey asked me to go with her over to Birch Point. She's teaching me to row! Maybe we'll find some late blackberries on the Point."

"Humph. Girls rowing. Young ladies should not be doing such things. And there'll be no blackberries left in early September, Sarah. Don't think I don't know that. I may be a foolish old woman, but I haven't yet lost my mind completely."

"Living close to the water, as we do, girls should learn how to row. Mr. Parsons said so. And with most of the young men gone to war … This is a new country, Mrs. Biddle. Women need to be able to take care of themselves."

"So you say, so you say. And what Betsey's family approves of is up to Betsey's family. What your mother would think, I cannot begin to guess. You must promise not to tell her I approved of your doing such things." Mrs. Biddle walked toward her bedchamber. "You've been good company to me these last weeks, and I'm truly glad you and that wild Betsey Parsons have become such good friends. Maybe you'll be a civilizing influence on her. Just be sure you're back by supper time." She turned, as Sarah was reaching for her bonnet. "Be certain to wear that bonnet every moment you're out of doors. And for heaven's sakes, girl, don't drown. What an embarrassment that would be for me to have to explain to your mother."

Sarah met Betsey, as they'd planned, down by the dock where the Parsons kept their small skiff.

"Did she give you any trouble about leaving?" asked Betsey.

"Oh, she always gives me a bit of trouble," said Sarah, "but as long as I do my chores she doesn't mind. I think underneath her complaints, I amuse her. And she likes the quiet time to take her naps in the afternoon. She says I'm noisy."

Betsey grinned. "If she thinks you're noisy, she should spend an hour at my house. She'd come away believing living with you was like living in a church." She gestured for Sarah to step into the skiff. "We almost had to take one of my sisters with us today. Ma was weary and everyone was clamoring for attention at home. I told her I'd promised you it would be just us, so she finally agreed."

"We could have taken Nabby or Kate."

"But then we couldn't have talked as freely, and would have had to watch them all the time. I deserve some time off, too." Betsy lifted her skirts higher than her mother would have approved and stepped into the skiff, reached to untie it, and pushed it away from the wharf with one of the oars. Then she settled herself in the center seat and began rowing. "I'll row first, if you don't mind."

"Go ahead. I'll watch. I'm curious to see the *Gruel*. How close are they to preparing her to sail?" Sarah asked.

"It's taken longer than anyone thought." Betsy angled the little boat and headed down river. "Pa's often said how much he appreciated your warning him about Reverend Bailey. If no one had mentioned the English knowing about the masts, he might not have moved the *Gruel* to a place where it's at least somewhat hidden."

The *Gruel* was now anchored near the shore of Cushman Cove, beyond Birch Point, almost hidden by Jeremy Squam Island and two points of land. At low tide it lay on the mud. As a further precaution, Mr. Parsons had ordered all the *Gruel*'s sails be removed and hidden on land, so no one could board her and sail away, and asked that Captain Proctor and her three crew members live on the ship, so the ship was never left alone.

The Wiscasset Militia had even moved a three-pound cannon from Wiscasset to the shore nearby, aimed in the direction of where an enemy ship would have to sail in order to reach the *Gruel*.

"It's a perfect place," Sarah agreed. "Near the lumberyard, and yet not out in the open where anyone could see her."

Betsey rowed closer. Captain Proctor waved at them from the deck and they waved back.

"It's been almost six weeks now. He must be ready to sail soon," said Sarah.

"Pa says the masts are close to finished, and they'll fill in the rest of the spaces with spars and shingles. He's already sent a message to Bath asking for two or three mariners to join the crew." Sarah turned the skiff toward Birch Point. "Your turn to row?"

Sarah nodded, and they carefully changed places.

"Keep the oars steady, as I've showed you," Betsey reminded her. "And straight up and down. Don't let them splash."

Each time Sarah rowed she got a little better at it. Rory would be surprised when he came home and found his little sister could manage a heavy skiff.

"Have you any word from Rory or Malcolm?" Betsey asked.

"No. We heard the British lost a battle near Bennington, Vermont, last month, but neither Rory nor Malcolm should have been there. I hope they're together. And I hope
they stay safe. Have you heard from Joseph?"

"Not since we got a letter saying his regiment was heading for Pennsylvania. What about your family in Boothbay?"

"All well. Jonathan brought a note from Mother last week. She misses everyone, and has some stomach complaints. Her major news is that she finally got some squash to grow in her garden. Admiral Collier has stayed away from Townsend Harbor for over a month now."

"Will you be returning soon?"

"Before the snows. I'll miss seeing ye, though, Betsey! Perhaps ye can come down river with Jonathan on one of his trips and visit Boothbay." Sarah struggled a bit with her left oar as the current grabbed it.

"You're doing fine," said Betsey, reaching to steady the oar. "I'd like to visit Boothbay. But Ma needs me to help with the children. Once this war ends and all the men come home we'll have more freedom."

"Let's hope that will be soon," said Sarah, giving both her oars a strong pull that sent the skiff up onto Birch Point. "So life can get back to normal, and we won't have to worry about battles and British soldiers and our brothers' safety."

Chapter 22
Stillwater, New York

Colonel Storer's militia and the other units traveling with it reached the east shore of the Hudson River just north of Albany the afternoon of September 6.

Ethan stared at the river in front of them. "I thought the Sheepscot River was wide. And the Kennebec. But the Hudson is wider than any Maine river I've seen."

"Word is we need to be on the west shore," said Rory. "The officers sent over to Albany for anything that will float to take us over."

Hundreds of weary men, plus their wagons and provisions all needed to cross.

It took two days, with small boats and rafts going back and forth across the Hudson day and night. As soon as a group of several hundred men was assembled on the west side of the river, an officer was assigned to march them north.

"General Gates is in charge of the American Army now," the word was passed, "and his forces are only thirty miles north of here, in a place called Stillwater."

Rory grinned at Ethan. "Since we've walked over three hundred miles since we left Falmouth, another thirty doesn't sound hard."

Ethan agreed. The men didn't notice their painful feet or empty stomachs or the cold morning fogs. Most had walked hundreds of miles to fight for their new nation, and they were finally going to do it.

As they approached Stillwater they heard the increasing din of wagons creaking, men shouting to each other, metal hitting metal, horses neighing, and cattle bellowing.

"Doesn't sound like a battle," said Ethan.

"If the British are as close as some say, there's no doubt they know where the American Army is," added Rory.

Stillwater had been a small hamlet of half a dozen homes. Now it was filled with thousands of men, tents, wagons, and animals. The York County men spilled out of their line into the small village, trying to absorb their first look at the army they had come to fight with.

Most of the men were white, but there were black faces in uniform, too. Some were as young as Rory and Ethan, but others were in their forties, or even older. Many, like the Maine men, did not wear uniforms. Others wore uniforms, although the colors differed, depending on the state and regiment they came from. Some uniforms were bright and new, but mmost could have used washing, or were faded, or torn. The soldiers carried muskets of various types over their shoulders, and linen haversacks, bags that held their food, knives, canteens, powder horns, and sometimes a knapsack for any spare clothing or personal possessions such as letters, or perhaps a razor. Despite months of living outdoors, most were clean-shaven.

Many soldiers were not speaking English. Rory recognized the Gaelic he'd heard in Scotland, here often spoken with an Irish lilt. Some soldiers were speaking German, some Dutch, and still others were speaking languages neither Rory nor Ethan recognized. There were women here, too, who'd followed the Army and were now helping load wagons with cooking pots, tents, blankets, and a few small, portable, ovens.

Some units were heading north, out of Stillwater, and it was clear the other regiments were preparing to follow them.

The loud "gee-haw!" ing of men and the heavy sound of cattle running through the center of Stillwater forced Rory and Ethan back toward the Hudson, where they saw the most amazing sight yet.

A bridge built of rafts stretched from one side of the Hudson River to the other, fully nine hundred feet long and sixteen feet wide. Soldiers stood along the edges of the bridge as hundreds of sheep and cattle were driven across from the east side.

Food was being delivered to the army.

"I wonder how long it took to build that!" said Rory.

"Pretty smart, eh?" said a soldier nearby, leaning on his musket. "The engineers' corps built that bridge. The company over there's been foraging, gathering food and information, and we'll get them all across and ready to join the rest of us in one day. I'm guessing we'll then destroy the bridge so the bloody Brits won't be able to use it."

"Who are they?" asked Rory, watching in fascination as the men lining the bridge yelled and poked at the animals with their musket stocks so the confused creatures didn't run off into the deep river.

"Part of the regiment that was Colonel Francis'," said the soldier. "From Massachusetts."

Rory grinned. "That's my cousin Malcolm's regiment! He's here!" Unless, Rory couldn't help thinking to himself, he'd been wounded. Or worse.

Chapter 23
Wiscasset, September 8

"Have ye noticed how well yer pumpkins are growing?" Sarah asked, as she filled the kettle with water. "They were hidden underneath all the high grasses Betsey and I cleared away."

Mrs. Biddle's special supply of tea leaves was now gone, so she'd been drinking a cup of hot water poured over mint leaves from her garden every morning.

"We have plenty of mint, since you uncovered it," she'd declared, "And it does settle my stomach. One must make do in these perilous times. Who knows how long it will be before I'll be able to get back home? No sane captain would sail the north seas in winter."

Sarah picked stalks of the mint leaves and hung them to dry in the kitchen. Mrs. Biddle would have several tin boxes filled for winter months. Reverend Bailey had visited three times, but had not brought news of a new parish for himself, or a way for Mrs. Biddle to leave Maine and return to England.

"You've been such a help to me, Sarah dear, and such good company. I had not realized how lonely I was," said Mrs. Biddle. "I will hate to lose you. Would you consider staying the winter?"

"I'm tempted, Mrs. Biddle," said Sarah truthfully, although most of the temptation lay in staying in Wiscasset, being able to see Betsey and being part of the excitement which hovered around the town and the Parsons family in particular. "But Mother has written that she misses me. Winters are long for her, too. If you're still here in the spring, perhaps I can visit, or return next summer."

"Oh, I dearly hope I am not still in this place next summer!" Mrs. Biddle pulled her black wool shawl around her tightly. "Already the fall breezes are too chilly for my old bones. I dread another hard winter here. And without my dear Mr. Biddle to keep me company and help keep the fire burning and my bones warm, my bed will be cold and my life dreary."

"Perhaps you could attend church Sundays," suggested Sarah, "Ye might meet people there who could become friends."

"Harrumph!" Mrs. Biddle replied. "I'm no Congregationalist, nor likely to be one. I'm an Anglican, same as my dear cousin. If his church were nearer, I would not hesitate to become an active member. But this New England religion is not mine, as I've told you, Sarah, many times."

"Ye have, indeed," said Sarah. "I was only suggesting, because I thought it would do you good to get out of this house and meet some people."

"People who would snigger and point at me and call me a Tory."

Sarah had no answer to that.

"I know what they say, Sarah. But at my age I'm not likely to change my opinions. I grew up when the world was one way, and that's the world I'm comfortable in. I'm not at peace in a country where rowdy colonists can take it into their minds to rule themselves, and not thank their betters, who've protected them and gotten them to where they are now. They're like children, growing up and then kicking the parents who raised them! No respect. These colonists have no respect for their king at all."

Sarah smiled. She'd heard it all before. Many times. There was no sense arguing.

But it was sad Mrs. Biddle had no friends in Wiscasset. Despite her loving England, which was home to her, she was a sweet old lady.

To Mrs. Biddle's surprise, Sarah reached over suddenly and hugged her. "I'm yer friend, and I won't be leaving ye for a while yet. I'll stay at least until the oak leaves are red. Sumac is the first to turn, and it's just beginning to change."

"Well," said Mrs. Biddle, a bit flustered by Sarah's sudden display of affection, "I do hope you stay until you get all the vegetables in from the garden. Every day it gets more difficult for me to bend over and cut those on the ground. I get dizzy, and my knees don't bend so well anymore."

A knock on the door interrupted them.

"Jonathan! Come in," Sarah gestured. "Mrs. Biddle, ye remember my friend Jonathan Decker who brought me here in July. He's the one who's been delivering letters from my family since." She turned to Jonathan. "Any messages for me today?"

"Yes, Sarah." Jonathan took off his hat and held it in his hands, and shuffled a bit. "Word for you, and for you, too, Mrs. Biddle. Sarah, I'm sorry to bring you the news that your mother, Mrs. Campbell, is doing poorly. Your uncle, Mr. Campbell, is worried about her health, and requests that you return to Boothbay to care for her."

"What is wrong with her? Has she asked fer me?" Sarah asked.

"She doesn't know he's sent for you," said Jonathan. "He said to tell you that particularly. And he said to apologize to you, especially, Mrs. Biddle, seeing as Sarah would be leaving sooner than planned. But he'd much appreciate her being at home."

"You'll go, of course, Sarah," said Mrs. Biddle. "If your mother needs you, you'll go."

Sarah nodded. "When are you returning to Boothbay, Jonathan?"

"I'd planned to go back in two days. But now I'm not as sure."

Jonathan looked at Sarah directly. "When I rounded the north end of Southport Island this morning I heard explosions. When I looked back I saw three of Admiral Collier's ships in Townsend Harbor. They were firing on Boothbay."

Chapter 24
Malcolm

Rory pushed his way through crowds of milling soldiers, trying to get closer to the men of Colonel Francis' regiment. Was Malcolm here? Was he still alive? Had he been wounded? Would he have changed in the months since he'd been in the army?

A harsh hand on his shoulder pulled Rory back. "Hey! You! Stop! Where are you going?"

"My cousin's with that regiment! I want to find him!" Rory shouted, trying to be heard above the crowd.

"Getting in the way of a herd of cattle's no way to find anyone," said the voice. "All regiments are pulling out, heading north."

Rory turned and looked at the soldier. "Yes, sir."

"You're with one of the militia, right?" asked the man.

"Yes, sir," said Rory.

The soldier sighed. "Every day more of you pour in from places I've never heard of. No doubt our numbers are growing, but how we're to feed everyone, only General Gates may know. Where is it you're from, boy?"

"District of Maine, sir."

"Where?"

"Eastern Massachusetts, sir. Just arrived today."

"Well, you tell whatever officer is in charge of your company, if he hasn't already heard, that we've orders to pull out and head north three miles to a place called Bemis Heights. Stay with your regiment and follow along and you'll find it. When everyone's there, and settled in, ask permission of your officer to look for your cousin. Never wander about without leave. You'll find the regiment you're seeking there easy enough. You can't just barge through military lines on your own."

"Aye, sir. I mean, no, sir."

The soldier smiled at Rory. "I hope you find your cousin well. And welcome to the Northern Army encampment. Some regulars give you militia men a hard time, but when it's time for fighting, we're glad you're here."

"Aye, sir. Thank you, sir," said Rory. He made his way back through the crowd. He'd find Colonel Storer and tell him what that soldier had said. Another three miles of marching.

Chapter 25
Sarah's Concerns

"If Admiral Collier was firing on Boothbay, then we have to tell the Wiscasset Militia to go there right now!" said Sarah. "He could have landed! He could have burned houses! People could be wounded, or dead!"

Jonathan looked at her and shook his head. "I left there early this morning. That was hours ago. By the time militia from Wiscasset could get down the river Collier's forces could have left. Or by now they could be halfway here."

Mrs. Biddle sat down hard on a chair and fanned herself. "Do you think the British might really come here? That they might fire on Wiscasset? They wouldn't know I'm on their side. Oh, I so wish I had a British flag I could raise! Oh, dear."

Sarah and Jonathan ignored her.

"Have you told Colonel Jones?" asked Sarah.

"You can be sure I rowed faster than I ever have. I went to him first thing. He didn't seem as concerned as I'd thought he'd be, but he did say he'd alert the men in his company." Jonathan shrugged his shoulders. "What else can be done?"

"The *Gruel*! Someone must alert Captain Proctor on the *Gruel*!" Sarah started pacing.

Jonathan grinned. "You're a fine Patriot girl, Sarah Campbell, to think of such things. But I'm sure Colonel Jones will do what is necessary."

"I must go back with you to Boothbay as soon as possible. I can pack my belongings in a few minutes." Sarah started for her chamber.

Jonathan put out his hand to stop her. "I won't leave for Boothbay until we're certain the river's clear. Not for at least two days, Sarah; perhaps three."

"But my mother is ill! And perhaps under attack! I must get to her."

"She does not know you've been sent for, and if the British are in Boothbay, or anywhere in the Sheepscot River, it will not help your mother to have you and I captured or our skiff overturned and us left on the shore miles from either Boothbay or Wiscasset."

"The young man is right, Sarah," put in Mrs. Biddle. "Take time to get your things ready to go. Perhaps you could prepare some mint to take to your mother. She once mentioned her stomach was bothering her. Mint is a great aid to the digestion."

"Jonathan, you must come and tell me the moment you hear any news from Boothbay. The very moment!" said Sarah. "Promise!"

"I promise, Sarah. I will. I'll be at Bradbury's, staying with a friend there. And I won't go back without you. But it may be a few days."

Sarah nodded. "I understand it appears that way now. But perhaps the situation will change."

"Perhaps," said Jonathan.

"Let us hope those British ships leave us in peace," said Mrs. Biddle. "My countrymen! How could they do anything that might have hurt your dear family, Sarah?"

Chapter 26
Encampment: September 9

Most of the march was along the River Road next to the Hudson. Beneath Bemis Heights soldiers had widened a narrow wagon path up a steep forested hill so their oxen and horses could pull supply wagons up onto the Heights. At first Rory and Ethan wondered why General Gates had chosen such a place for an encampment.

But when they reached the top, two hundred feet above the Hudson, they knew. They could see for miles up and down the river. Between the river and the Heights were hills covered with thick forests of oak trees and maples and tall elms, and pines that stood, starkly green, within the dense foliage.

Rory'd thought the Highlands in Scotland beautiful, but this was his country now. He'd seen more of it in the past month than he'd known existed. America was beautiful, farmland or mountain, river or shore. And there was space enough here for everyone. Even the most crowded cities were only a little over a hundred years old.

A young country. A free country. The men here were so varied, but all had come far to fight for what they believed in. A chance to be a part of a country where a man could make his own future.

If they fought well, Dan's son Liberty would grow up in a country where men would no longer have to fight for freedom.

"The red jackets the British wear will be easy enough to see long before they get close enough to shoot," said Ethan, bringing Rory back to today. "No one can sneak up on us here on the Heights."

"Perhaps if they marched up the road by the river, or up the trail we just took. But anyone could be hiding in these woods," said Rory, doubtfully. "The trees are so close together, and the hills so steep, how could we see them approaching?"

"The British fight in lines and groups," said Ethan. "There's no place here for a battle like that except in the fields farmers have cleared. And those are filled with stumps. Besides, our soldiers could hide behind trees, too."

"Perhaps," agreed Rory.

By nightfall General Gates had established his headquarters in a small farmhouse owned by Captain Woodsworth, and the regiments of the Northern Department of the Continental Army and the various militias which had joined them had set up their camps on the land surrounded by dense forests.

Areas were set aside for the officers' horses, and for the horses and oxen that pulled the supply wagons. Ethan and Rory were first assigned to help fence in an area for the sheep and cattle.

After the animals were contained, they helped establish the small part of the camp designated for Colonel Storer's regiment. The regular army had tents, but the militias had to build small huts out of whatever downed trees and boards and brush they could find.

Rory and Ethan shared a hut with three other men: crusty old Nathaniel Pritcher from Wells, Ira Smollett from Falmouth, and Seth Turner from Weymouth. The five men stood their muskets outside their hut so they leaned against each other, forming a triangle. There they'd stay dry, and be easy to reach.

Dinner was boiled beans and fresh beef, which was more than they'd had in days. Most important, they'd finally reached the goal they'd had when they'd enlisted. They were now with the Continental Army, and the work they'd done that day was supporting the needs of their new nation.

When it was dusk, and the men had started to settle down in their new quarters, Rory looked for the captain of his company.

"Sir, I'd like permission to look for my cousin. He's serving with the 11th Massachusetts, in Colonel Francis's regiment.

The captain smiled at him. "Permission granted, Campbell. Although I understand there are now seven thousand regular Army soldiers here, plus almost two thousand militia men, with more arriving every day. It may take you a while to find your cousin."

"Yes, sir," said Rory, turning to leave.

"I believe the Massachusetts regiments are in General Paterson's area of the field," added the captain. "You might start there."

Rory wandered from one camp to another. The encampment covered almost a full square mile. Some units had raised their colors over their sites. General Gates' headquarters flew the Continental flag: thirteen red stripes alternated with white, representing the thirteen colonies that had signed the Declaration of Independence the year before.

Rory looked up at it proudly. "Thirteen *states*," he said to himself. "We are colonies no more."

Most of the regiments were from New York, New Hampshire, and Massachusetts, but units of riflemen were from Virginia and Pennsylvania. Militias were from Vermont, New Hampshire, Connecticut, and New York as well as Massachusetts. One Continental unit was made up of men from Canada.

Rory had never seen so many men together at one time. How could they fail to defeat the British?

Everywhere he saw Massachusetts men he asked, "Is this the regiment that served under Colonel Francis?"

Finally, he found them. "I'm looking for Malcolm Campbell, sir," he asked a soldier standing near the front of their encampment. The soldier looked him up and down. "And what would you be wanting with him, then?"

Rory smiled. The man must know Malcolm, or he'd not be asking. "I'm his cousin, from the District of Maine."

"Hey, Campbell! Out with ya!" shouted the soldier toward the opening of the tent nearest to him. "Seems ye've got yerself a visitor from home!"

Within seconds Malcolm appeared, tucking in his shirt, and looking a bit dazed; apparently he'd been sleeping. He looked at Rory, and then looked again.

"I canna believe my eyes. Rory? Is it really you?"

"Aye. Truly. In the flesh!" Rory grinned. And for the first time in their lives the cousins hugged each other.

"What are ye doing here?" asked Malcolm, drawing Rory over to the side, and finding space on a blanket for them to sit. "How did ye get here? How is everyone? Talk to me!"

"I'm in the 3rd York Militia," Rory said proudly. "Everyone was well when I left home in early August. Sarah was staying with a woman in Wiscasset for the summer, and all was the same in Boothbay."

"How ever did ye get Father to let ye enlist? Yer still a lad!" said Malcolm.

"I'm fourteen!" said Rory. "To be truthful," he lowered his voice, "I ran away. A sloop was leaving for Falmouth, and they'd called out for militia to help after Ticonderoga so … I came."

"And Father and yer Mother dinna know!" Malcolm roared with laughter. "Rory, my lad ye've grown up fast since I enlisted. They've no doubt been praying fer yer body and soul ever since ye left. But ye got here." He looked at Rory again and reached over to rumple his hair, much to Rory's embarrassment. "It's good to see ye."

"So, what was it like at Ticonderoga? What happened? How did the British win?"

Malcolm shook his head. "It wasna a pretty picture. We were outnumbered by the thousands. Burgoyne had over nine thousand troops, they said, including those Germans he has fighting fer him, and the Indians on their side. We had only four thousand, with more men sick and weak from the measles than ye can imagine. General St. Clair decided it was best if we left Ticonderoga, and saved ourselves and our weapons to fight at a better time and place. We snuck out in the middle of the night, and left the fort to the British."

"You just left! You didn't even fight!"

"Not then. But we did soon enough after. Colonel Francis – as fair and fine an officer as ever a man would want to serve under – was in command of the rear guard, and I was in one of the companies with him. Troops started leaving the fort at two in the morning July 6, carrying what they could, and marching south. We were to wait until all had gotten safely on their way to Fort Edward, and then delay Burgoyne's forces if they followed."

"And did they follow?" Rory asked.

"Aye, for sure they did. That first day we didn't see them. You understand, the trail we took was a rough one. Up hills, like the ones you see here, and down valleys, with only space for two men to walk, and deep ruts in the road. Not easy marching, for certain. And we were the rear guard, along with some fine Green Mountain men – they're from Vermont – and men from New Hampshire. But we also had several hundred of the men who'd been sick or wounded; well enough to walk, but not strong enough to keep up with their companies. Those stragglers slowed us down some."

"But ye couldn't leave them by the side of the road," said Rory.

"No, we couldna. They were our brothers in arms. Colonel Hale, from New Hampshire, had charge of those poor souls, and did his best to keep them going. That first day we walked nine or ten hours in the steaming July heat on those crude pathways through the wilderness. Twenty miles we walked." Malcolm shook his head. "Some of us might have been able to keep going, but others for sure could not. We'd been awake all night the night before, and needed to stop."

"And so?"

"We came to a place called Hubbardton, where there was a small field, and a hill, offering some protection, should the British overtake us — for we were sure they were somewhere behind — and a brook. Tired as we were, we felled trees and put up barricades along the brook before making camp for the night."

"And did the British find you?"

"Aye, they did. Our men who were hidden above the road to alert us when they saw the first of the British troops began firing at dawn. That's when we took our positions at the brook."

"Were there many of them?"

"Enough. It was General Fraser's men. Ye'll hear talk of him, Rory. A fellow Scot, from Inverness, and very well thought of by General Burgoyne. If he were on our side, he'd be one of our best. But he's with them, and his men attacked with force, up the hill to our fortifications. Two times we drove them back. But the third time …. the third time they charged with bayonets. We ran, across a wheat field and up another hill and into the woods, where there was some shelter, and we could turn and fight again." Malcolm paused.

"Aye? And then?" said Rory.

"That's where Colonel Francis himself fell. Shot in the arm first, and kept on going, but then shot through the chest." Malcolm stopped. "I didn't see him, but my friend Jed, he did. But there was no time to reach him. We began to attack again, but then the

German troops arrived, as though from nowhere, with their band playing and singing hymns."

"Singing hymns!" said Rory, listening to every word.

"Drilling and marching prepares ye in some ways. But nothing prepares ye for real battles," said Malcolm.

"So who won?"

"I'd say the British did, although they lost men, for sure," said Malcolm. "But they stopped following General St. Clair's forces, and our army was able to get to Fort Edward safely. A rear guard's mission is to delay those following, and, aye, we did that. But we lost Colonel Francis and other fine men in the doing."

"And since then?"

"August 16 there was a battle near Bennington. Burgoyne sent a detachment of German troops to forage for food and supplies. Word reached us he was running low on both. He believed there were Tories in Vermont who would help him, but instead the Germans met up with militia units from Vermont and New Hampshire that defeated them soundly. The Brits lost nine hundred men there I've heard."

"I wish I could have been there!" said Rory.

"You'll get your chance. For two months Burgoyne has followed us south. We spent the summer felling trees and brush and destroying bridges. Trying to make the trails behind us impassable. But they're now only a few miles north of here. Time for running has ended. It's time again for fighting," said Malcolm.

"Then I haven't missed the battle!" said Rory.

"No, cousin," said Malcolm. "You haven't that. I only hope we'll be celebrating together when it's over."

Chapter 27
Wiscasset, Early Morning, September 10

Sarah's sleep was interrupted by dreams of houses burning. Houses in Falkirk; houses in Boothbay. She woke again and again, certain she smelled the smoke that had smoldered for days after her home had burned. Screams, and her mother's sobs, echoed in her head.

All she could think of was her new home in Boothbay, perhaps now in flames from gunpowder and cannon fire, burning as her home in Scotland had burned.

She got up, afraid to face any more dreams. The night was dark, the moon covered by clouds and fog.

Rory had always been the one to have nightmares; not Sarah. Where was Rory now? Had he enlisted in the militia, as he'd planned? Had he reached the army? She'd heard Fort Ticonderoga had fallen, and there'd been a battle at a place called Hubardton. Was Malcolm all right?

Too many questions without answers. Why couldn't this war end and leave them in peace?

Sarah threw her shawl over her shoulders and went out into the back yard, shivering in the mid-September chill. The fog was so heavy she couldn't see the outline of Bradbury's Inn on the next block, or Betsey's house across from it.

An owl screeched in the darkness. All else was silent.

Would night never end?

She was almost ready to go inside and try again to sleep when she heard heavy footsteps. Someone was running on Fort Hill Street, and then pounding on a door.

"Mr. Parsons! Mr. Parsons! Wake up!"

Sarah walked to the back of the yard, as close as she could get to the Parsons' home. Why would someone wake Mr. Parsons before dawn? A problem at the lumberyard?

Whoever was pounding continued to knock and yell. Finally Mr. Parsons answered. Sarah couldn't hear his voice, but she heard the first man clearly.

"Get the militia! Quickly! Colonel Jones won't answer my calls! The British have brought two longboats up the river. They're on the *Gruel*! They've stolen our cannon, and taken Captain Proctor and his men prisoner!"

Sarah ran inside and dressed quickly. What could she do to help?

But, she couldn't help thinking, at least the British weren't in Boothbay anymore.

Chapter 28
The Working Army

Loud drums and twittering fifes woke Rory early the next morning. He rubbed his eyes and jumped up. His clothes were wet and cold with fog. Even his blanket hadn't helped.

Colonel Storer called his men together. "The British are only seven miles north of here. We have no time to waste. General Gates' scouts are tracking their movements, and no doubt they have scouts tracking ours. Colonel Kosciuszko, a military engineer from Poland, has designed fortifications for our encampment critical to our defense."

Malcolm had been right. The battle would be soon. Rory strained to hear every word.

"Our job is to aid in building a chest-high wall we can stand behind while we fire. The breastworks will be three-sided, each side three quarters of a mile long, on the top of the Heights, with a battery in the center and at each corner for our cannons. We must dig trenches, line them horizontally with trees from the forests to our rear, and then pack earth between the trees to create a solid wall of defense. We have more men than tools. Trade off axes or shovels in half hours. Other forces will be building defenses above the river and near the foot of Bemis Heights. Remember – the British are near.

Our lives may depend on what we build today."

Ethan and Rory were first assigned to carry loads of heavy iron shovels from a supply wagon near the edge of the forest. "Even with thousands of men, how can we be expected to dig a trench and then build a wall 3/4 of a mile long?" grumbled Ethan. "It sounds impossible."

Rory shook his head. "I don't know."

"We didn't think we'd be chopping down trees and digging instead of shooting, did we?" asked Ethan, as they made their way across the campsites to the wagon. "Feels like I'm back on the farm in Wiscasset."

"From what my cousin told me last night, being in the army isn't all shooting. One of the other militia units is digging latrines. At least we didn't get that duty today," answered Rory. He stopped and pointed at several tents and a wagon near a barn. "What's that area?"

"While you were with your cousin last night, I was looking about myself," said Ethan. "That's the hospital, where surgeons, mates and women are caring for soldiers."

"Wounded soldiers?" asked Rory. "There hasn't been a battle yet."

"Not wounded. But with this many men, some are bound to have ailments of some sort. I saw one man who'd cut his foot with an ax. And the hospital will be there when it's needed."

The boys looked at each other. Neither wanted to talk about battle wounds. Not now. Not so close to the time a battle would be real.

"One soldier I spoke with, Private Steiner, from Connecticut, said the Continental Army has lost more men to smallpox then they have to bullets." Ethan looked over at Rory. "Have you had the pox?"

"When I was a baby, in Scotland. Most in our village had it."

"I had it in Wiscasset. But I told Seth and Ira, and they haven't been exposed. They said they were going to stay clear of the medical area," said Ethan. "Seth said he didn't want to be one of those who goes to war to fight and dies of fever."

"Is there pox here now?"

"No. But it was in Boston, Steiner said, and killed men in the Quebec campaign. And there was measles at Ticonderoga. General Gates ordered extra medical supplies, on the chance there are epidemics here."

Chapter 29
Sarah and Betsey Sound the Alarm

Sarah rapped on Mrs. Biddle's bedchamber door and then opened it slightly. "Mrs. Biddle, I'm running to the Parsons' house to see if I can be of help. British forces have sailed up the river and are on the *Gruel*. They've already stolen the cannon near there."

"Goodness gracious, girl," said Mrs. Biddle, her nightcap falling awry as she rose from under her quilts. "Did you say the British had come up the Sheepscot? Today?"

"I heard someone shouting. I don't know details yet. I'm going to find out. I'll be back later."

Sarah didn't stop to hear Mrs. Biddle's reply. She ran down the street to the Parsons' house. Their door was open. Mr. Parsons was dressed and about to leave, his musket slung over his shoulder. Sarah had never before seen him with a weapon.

"Sarah! What are you doing here at this hour?"

"I was in Mrs. Biddle's yard, and heard that man knocking on your door and calling to you. Is it true? Have the British taken the *Gruel*?"

"They haven't taken it yet, girl, but they've boarded. They hadn't planned on its not being equipped with sails."

Mrs. Parsons and Betsey entered the room, both fully dressed.

Ben followed. He also carried a musket.

Mr. Parsons looked at all of them. "Good. We can use all of your help. Colonel Jones should have alerted the militia, but he was sleeping too soundly to be awakened. perhaps he overindulged in rum last night. But with him or without him, we need all the men and muskets we can get. We've already lost our cannon. We have to let those Brits know they can't sail into Wiscasset and take what they want."

"What can we do?" asked Betsey.

"I'm going out to Birch Point. You go with me, Ben. We'll wake the men who live out that way and secure the lumberyard and all the lumber left in it. If we have to burn it to keep it out of British hands, we will." He turned to Sarah and Betsey. "You two, go from door to door in Wiscasset. The militia should be the ones responding but, tarnation! This is a town issue. Wake everyone! Tell them what's happened, and direct every man to get to Birch Point as soon as possible. Tell them to bring any weapons or ammunition they have."

"We'll show those British!" said Betsey, putting on her bonnet and shawl.

"Who was it who woke you this morning?" Sarah asked Mr. Parsons. She realized that in her haste she'd left her bonnet behind, but she wasn't going to return for it now. Not even for propriety's sake.

"The *Gruel*'s cook," said Mr. Parsons, smiling a bit. "He snuck off the ship late last night to visit a lady friend, and was planning to sneak back before dawn this morning. When he got to the shore he saw the two British longboats, sailors on board the *Gruel*, and the cannon gone. I've sent him to wake the sexton to ring the church bell. Now – off with you two!"

"You take the north side of Main Street; I'll take the south side," Sarah suggested.

Betsey nodded, and they both ran. As Sarah saw Betsey's skirts disappearing into the heavy fog the church bells began to toll, over, and over, and over. New England church bells only rang like that in an emergency.

Chapter 30
Challenges of Freedom

"What's happening over there?" Rory and Ethan, weary after days of digging trenches and chopping down trees, were slumped on the ground after another supper of beans.

The fortifications were far from finished, and they were exhausted.

But every day new militias climbed the path into camp. They'd come to offer help. They could shoot, and they were willing to fight for liberty.

The word that General Gates was asking for more men was still filtering through the countryside. Men were still responding.

But tonight something else was happening.

"Let's go and see," said Ethan.

The problem, for problem it clearly was, was within one unit of the New Hampshire militia.

"We signed up to serve two months. The two months is up at midnight, and we're going home," one man yelled.

"My wife is with child. I promised her I'd serve no longer than need be," shouted another. "You can't make me stay!"

"Two months! Two months! Two months!" The chant rose from all over the militia's camp.

General Gates himself was deep in discussion with the officer in charge of the unit. ("That's John Stark. He was the hero of the Battle of Bennington!" one New Hampshire man pointed out proudly. "He'll do well by us!")

Finally Stark held up his arms. The men quieted down. "Men! General Gates has asked us to stay on. He says the battle could be hours from now, and every man and musket from New Hampshire will be needed."

"Home! Now!" yelled one man.

"We've served our time!" shouted another.

"General Gates is generously offering any man who stays the sum of ten dollars," Stark added.

"He can't buy me! I'm leavin' tonight!"

"We don't answer to General Gates! We answer to New Hampshire!"

"I'm with you!"

Voices came from all over the regiment.

"Do ye really think they'll go?" Rory asked quietly. "The British are only a few miles away. The battle could be any time. Everyone says it'll be this week, fer sure."

Ethan shook his head in disbelief. "They look determined to leave."

"We signed up fer three months," said Rory. "Would our unit walk away right before a battle if the three months were over?"

Ethan paused. "I hope not."

They stood and watched as the men milled about, packing their belongings into knapsacks and bags, and lining up. At the stroke of midnight, John Stark and his six hundred New Hampshire Militiamen marched down off Bemis Heights and headed back to New Hampshire.

General Gates now had eight thousand and seven hundred men, minus six hundred, to fight the British.

Chapter 31
Wiscasset Patriots and the *Gruel*

The church bell was still tolling, and dawn was beginning to burn through the heavy fog that enveloped Wiscasset and its harbor.

Sarah pounded on the first door she came to. A sleepy old man wearing a shirt but still buttoning his breeches opened it. "The British are on the *Gruel*!" she told him. "Everyone who has a musket is to come to Birch Point!" The man didn't ask questions; his mouth tightened, and he nodded.

At almost every door Sarah got the same response. Most people had already been wakened by the church bells and knew something was wrong.

She spoke the words, "The British are on the *Gruel*!" to old men and young, to women; to children. Most young men had enlisted in the army or militia and were far from home. Those still in Wiscasset were for the most part the old, the young, and the women.

At the Bradbury Inn the old man Sarah remembered from the kitchen kindly volunteered to tell those sleeping there. By the time she had nearly finished knocking on her share of Wiscasset's doors, men, women, and children were passing her, many of the adults carrying muskets, heading for the waterfront, and Birch Point.

Sarah ran back to Mrs. Biddle's home. "Mrs. Biddle! I'm going with the rest of the townspeople, over to Birch Point."

"I've heard the church bells ringing and seen people running. What do you all think you can do? Stop the King's Navy?" Mrs. Biddle was dressed in her best black dress and holding a flowered bonnet.

Sarah grinned. "We can try!"

To Sarah's astonishment, Mrs. Biddle tied her bonnet tightly beneath her ample chins. "That I have to see. I'm going with you, Sarah Campbell. I'm not going to stay at home and miss the most exciting thing that's happened in this town since I've lived here!"

Mrs. Biddle walked surprisingly quickly as Sarah took her arm and they headed for the waterfront.

Of course, Sarah realized. Walking to Birch Point would take hours, especially for the children and older people. Going by water would take only minutes. It appeared everyone in Wiscasset who'd hidden a small vessel of some sort had pulled it out, and was now rowing or sailing across to the point. A fleet of small vessels filled the waters between Wiscasset and Birch Point.

"Sarah Campbell!"

She turned around. Jonathan was there, with several of his friends. "Sarah, would you like a ride to the Point? I have my skiff."

"I'm with Mrs. Biddle. Have you room for both of us?" asked Sarah, looking at Jonathan's small skiff.

Jonathan hesitated, as he looked at the ample Mrs. Biddle.

"I can take one oar," Sarah declared. "And after we take her, I'll help you come back and we can take others across."

Jonathan grinned. "Sarah Campbell, you can row?"

"Certainly, she can!" said Mrs. Biddle. "Young women do what must be done!"

Jonathan shook his head. "You Campbells are full of surprises." He shrugged. "Mrs. Biddle, your vessel awaits you." He helped her in, and then handed the oars to Sarah, who was already in the skiff, and pushed off. "I'll be right back to take you over!" he called to his friends on shore as he climbed on board.

He and Sarah went back and forth five times, as did several other small boats, until there was no one left standing on the Wiscasset waterfront.

By mid-morning most of the citizens of Wiscasset above the age of ten, and some under, were standing or sitting on the shore of Birch Point. About a third of them were holding muskets pointed toward the *Gruel*.

It was mid-tide, and the *Gruel* listed toward the shore. The British sailors on board had taken wood from below decks and built a wall of lumber on the shore side of the ship's deck to protect them from bullets. But they had no way of escaping.

They couldn't sail away. They had no sails.

"My dear Sarah," said Mrs. Biddle, who was sitting on the shore, clearly enjoying the scene. "Whatever do you think is going to happen next? Those young men on the ship can't sit there forever."

"Something will happen," said Sarah. "I'm sure of it. Maybe they'll just get back in their longboats and go back to their ship."

"That's the puzzle," said Mrs. Biddle. "Surely they didn't come all the way up the Sheepscot River in those two little boats? They must have a ship somewhere."

Mrs. Biddle was right. At almost exactly noon the fog cleared completely and Admiral Collier's frigate, the 44-gun *HMS Rainbow*, sailed around Jeremy Squam Island and cast anchor in Wiscasset Harbor.

Chapter 32
The American Camp: September 19

The day dawned dark and foggy, as almost every morning seemed to on Bemis Heights.

As usual, Rory woke to the sound of drums. But this morning the drums' sound was echoed through the hills. He rolled over and shoved Ethan. "Listen! The drums sound different!"

Ethan sat up, and so did the other men in the hut. Seth was the first to figure it out. "It's British drums we're hearing. They're close, and the winds must be right, so we hear drums waking soldiers in their camp."

The men hurriedly got up, but no one had more information. The fog was thick; not even the Hudson was visible from the Heights. The soldiers were edgy. Everyone sensed this day would be different from yesterday.

No one told them anything directly. Generals were the ones to receive intelligence. But when the fog burned off, word passed quickly that American scouts a mile north of camp had seen the bright red of British uniforms through the foliage. British troops were climbing the steep ravine north of Bemis Heights, and German units were on the road by the river.

All over the American camp, men in uniforms and men in worn

homespun were cleaning their muskets and checking their powder horns and cartridges boxes. Waiting.

General Gates conferred with his generals. Soldiers watched as scouts, on foot and on horseback, came and went to the small house where decisions were being made. They knew the battle would be fought soon.

Captains shouted orders. Drums rolled. Fifes sang. Women and children were sternly ordered to get to the back of the camp, out of the way. Every man stood at attention in his unit, ready.

Rory stood with the others, his musket over his shoulder. His arm cramped from holding it so stiffly. Small fragments of fog still hung in the air, like torn remnants of a scene that had been painted over. It was like a dream. But it was real.

As his company stood, awaiting the command to go somewhere, do something, do anything, a new militia company walked up the hill from the road to Albany. "Is this where you volunteer to fight for the revolution?" asked the man at the front of the new line. "We've come to do our part."

One regiment of riflemen and one of light artillery were sent west and north, on paths through heavy stands of pines and oaks and maples, to see how close the British were.

Rory heard the first shots at about one in the afternoon. Musket fire, then cannon fire. The men turned to each other. Who was shooting? The cannon must be British; no American cannons were near where the sounds were coming from.

"Let us at 'em!" someone shouted. "Why should other men have all the fun?"

"Simmer down!" yelled Colonel Storer in reply. "We'll be called when needed."

The shooting continued. Next to Rory, Ethan counted the beats it took the soldiers to reload. They could almost see the men, firing, stopping to reload, and firing again. Then another cannon would thunder.

"There's men being killed out there," said a man in back of Rory. "We're standing here. Just standing here, while men're dying!"

"We came here to fight, not listen!" said another.

Where was Malcolm? Had General Paterson's men been sent to where the shooting was? Rory had no way of knowing.

Several red-coated soldiers were dragged out of the forest and pushed toward General Gates' headquarters. "Look!" He pointed them out to Nathaniel. "They must have captured some of the lobsterbacks and are taking them in to find out what they know."

A few minutes later more regiments headed off through the woods.

Colonel Storer looked frustrated, too. No word had come for them as yet.

Then all was quiet. The men not yet sent to fight were told to sit down. Save their energy.

"What's happening?" Rory whispered to Ethan. "Is the battle over?"

"I don't know. Maybe. Or maybe they've moved somewhere else. Somewhere we can't hear them."

Men ran back and forth from the forest to General Gates' headquarters. A few men carried wounded comrades out of the woods and took them to the barn that served as a hospital.

Rory tried not to look closely at the men whose clothing was ripped and stained with blood, and whose limbs dangled at unnatural angles. They were far enough away so they, like the tufts of fog earlier, did not look real. They could be visions. Or nightmares.

Suddenly, at 3:40 by Colonel Storer's pocket watch, the battle erupted again, with muskets cracking and cannon fire louder than before.

"The British must have moved in more guns," said Ethan.

"They're all firing together."

Rory could hardly hear Seth's voice. What would it like to be in the middle of the fighting? To hear muskets firing all around you, and cannons blasting. He tried not to think about what you'd be seeing. For sure you'd be smelling and tasting the smoke of the guns and the cannons.

Thick, dark smoke, like the smoke in Falkirk. The smoke here would kill men, too. More men than that smoke in Scotland.

Suddenly Rory couldn't breathe.

He stood up.

"Where are you going?" asked Ethan. "We're supposed to stay here. We could be called to duty at any moment."

"I need air," Rory said, quickly, shaking his head. Ethan wouldn't understand. "I'll be back."

He ran from his company toward where Malcolm's unit had been waiting. If he saw Malcolm, saw someone from his family, well, and healthy, maybe the visions would go away. He ran past three other militia units, waiting, as his regiment was.

He ran past two regiments of regular soldiers.

He ran until he came to where Malcolm's company had been waiting.

Wildly, he looked around. Where was Malcolm?

An older man came up to him and touched his shoulder. "Are you all right, boy?"

"I'm looking for my cousin. Malcolm Campbell. He should be here, with this unit!"

"Not today, lad. Your cousin's one of the best. He was chosen to serve in Henry Dearborn's light infantry today. They've been called to battle, son. They're gone."

Chapter 33

Admiral Collier in Wiscasset Harbor

The people of Wiscasset stood on Birch Point and watched as the *HMS Rainbow*, frigate of the dreaded Admiral Collier who'd been looting and burning towns all along the coast of Maine, dropped anchor in their harbor.

"I do hope they won't burn Wiscasset," said Mrs. Biddle. "I wish I could talk to those men, so they'd know there are loyal British citizens in this town."

Somewhere in back of her a man laughed.

About a dozen of the local militiamen started firing their muskets at the deck of the *Gruel,* hoping to hit one of its British captors.

Mothers quickly took their children further back on shore, and hid behind trees. Everyone waited to see what would happen. But no one on the *Gruel* fired back.

Then a longboat was slowly lowered from the deck of the *Rainbow.* Several people were on board. One sailor was waving a white flag.

"Huh! I don't believe they're surrendering. No doubt they just want to chat," said one woman. "Do they think they can talk us into giving them the *Gruel* and everything on board her?"

"If they think that, they'd better think again," another voice spoke up.

"If they want to talk to someone, then I guess they can talk to me," said a tall thin man standing in the middle of all the commotion. "Jonathan Decker, your skiff is close at hand. Would you row me out to where those Brits are?"

"Yes, sir!" said Jonathan, who pushed off his skiff, and picked up his oars.

"I wish he'd asked me to help," said Sarah. "Who is that tall man, anyway?"

"That's Tom Rice, the first selectman," said the woman next to Mrs. Biddle. "Nice sort of man, in his way. Harmless, I'd say. With most of the men off to war, he's the closest person we've got to an official in charge of Wiscasset, so probably he's the one that English admiral should talk to. But I do hope the admiral doesn't yell too loud. Tommy doesn't like people to yell at him."

"Oh, dear," said Mrs. Biddle. "Maybe they should have asked me to talk to him. I'd know how to talk sense into a decent Englishman."

They watched as Jonathan rowed Mr. Rice out toward the longboat.

The two boats stayed together for some time. Clearly negotiations of some sort were going on.

Once in a while a Wiscasset militiamen would fire a shot toward the *Gruel,* as though to remind everyone that this *was* a war.

Otherwise, all was quiet.

"In truth, this is getting a bit wearisome," said Mrs. Biddle.

Some children played tag. Women chatted in groups. Since nothing dangerous had happened so far, there was a feeling of bravado in the crowd. Everyone was treating the British taking over the *Gruel* as a sort of holiday, although they all knew that at any time Admiral Collier could decide to turn his forty-four cannons on Wiscasset and burn the town, as Captain Mowatt had burned Falmouth, and as Admiral Collier had fired on Boothbay.

The Admiral might even turn his guns directly on the townspeople at Birch Point.

But instead of cannon or musket fire there were just those two small boats in the harbor, with the dreaded Admiral Collier and tall thin Tom Rice, talking.

Finally the two boats separated, and Jonathan rowed Mr. Rice back to Birch Point.

"Gather 'round!" He called out. "Fellow friends and neighbors! I assure you I've negotiated with all my best skills and judgments. You will be pleased to know that Admiral Collier has agreed to take no hostile actions until tomorrow."

"What! And THEN he is going to burn our town!" said one woman. "Tommy Rice, you go right back out there and negotiate some more. That is NOT acceptable!"

"Well, he wanted us to give him the *Gruel* and everything on it. I didn't agree to that!" said Mr. Rice.

"Well, of course you didn't! But he can't sail the *Gruel* away without sails, and it's on mud most of the time in any case, so he can't even tow it away. And we have his sailors. Did he say how many of his sailors are on the *Gruel*, Tommy?"

"Forty, he said."

"Then we have forty of his sailors hostage on our ship. So it seems he'd better be giving US something if he wants his sailors back. Don't you think so?"

"I hadn't thought of it like that," said Mr. Rice. He looked out toward the *HMS Rainbow*. "But the Admiral has gone back to his ship. Maybe I'll talk with him again tomorrow."

"Tomorrow!" the frustrated woman threw up her hands. "We could all be blown to bits by tomorrow!"

Sarah looked at Mrs. Biddle. "I guess nothing exciting is going to happen today."

"I think we've had enough excitement in any case. Some of those men with muskets had better stay out here for the night, but the rest of us might just as well go home," agreed Mrs. Biddle. "Do you think your friend Jonathan would row me back to town? It's almost time for supper."

Chapter 34
After the Battle

Malcolm was on the battlefield.

Rory stood still. He had to return to his own unit. He had to. He talked to himself the way he sometimes did when he woke from a nightmare. He told himself the smoke and fire were only in his mind.

Except that the air on Bemis Heights was becoming black with smoke, even this far from the battle lines, and his ears hurt from the thundering of the cannons.

Slowly, carefully, one step at a time, he walked back to where the 3rd York was still waiting.

This was what he'd wanted to do. This was why he had left his family and come all these miles.

Silently he took his place in the line.

"Are you all right?" asked Ethan.

He nodded. "Aye. I am now."

The musket fire and cannons continued. Rory tried not to think of what was happening on the other side of those dense woods. What was happening to Malcolm?

At 5:00 the noise became even more intense. Added to the cacophony of the battle was the beating of many drums. More men were running and riding back and forth to General Gates' headquarters. It was early evening when "The Hessian Regiments, the Germans, are now on the field" was the word passed quickly among those remaining in camp.

No one in Rory's company said anything. They had not been asked to take part. They had not been wanted.

The battle went on until nightfall.

After dark, soldiers began to stumble back into camp, many of them carrying wounded friends. Colonel Storer ordered his men to search the woods and field near where the battle had taken place, and bring the dead and wounded back to camp.

Rory and Ethan and Seth searched together, hoping, and yet not hoping, to find bodies. They found one man who'd bled to death after his arm had been shot off. Another whose face no one would be able to recognize.

Ethan threw up in the underbrush when they picked up one man and his hand fell off.

At least it was dark; they couldn't see a lot of the details.

All around them the moaning of the wounded, American and British, filled the cold night air, mixed with the howling of wolves. Wolves who smelled blood. The temperature was below freezing. The men waiting to be found were shivering with cold and pain.

Back at the camp, exhausted men who'd fought that day slept on their arms, ready to jump up and fight again at a moment's notice. Others did what they could for the wounded after they'd been brought to the hospital barn. Dozens of soldiers dug mass graves.

They worked all night, but the groaning in the woods and on the field where the battle had been fought, a field that had once grown corn and wheat for the Freeman family, continued. It would take another day to find all the dead and injured.

As another cold foggy day dawned, Rory and Seth helped a young soldier from New Hampshire who'd been shot badly through the leg hobble to the hospital area. The barn had long since been filled. The wounded lay on straw outside the building.

"Thank you kindly," said the soldier, as the boys helped him to the ground. "You done me a great service. Now the wolves and vultures won't get to me."

"I wish you well," said Rory. He straightened up. He and Seth had just been relieved of their duty; they could now sleep briefly, waiting to find out whether the battle would resume again. Whether this would be the day they would be called to fight. Whether tomorrow morning it would be their bodies that would be carried to one of the mass graves, or to the hospital.

"Rory? Rory? Is that you?"

He turned, and looked around.

Malcolm was lying on the ground, not ten feet away.

Chapter 35

Wiscasset in Danger

Sarah didn't sleep much that night. Not many in Wiscasset did. Admiral Collier had promised he wouldn't take any action until the next day.

But when would that next day begin? At midnight? At dawn? And what would the action be? Burning the town? Shooting the Wiscasset men who'd volunteered to stay on Birch Point all night?

Once in a while a musket shot or two rang out through the darkness, but Sarah suspected they were only reminder shots from the men on shore near the *Gruel*. All else was quiet.

As soon as it was light she, and most of the townspeople, went to the waterfront to see if anything had changed. To their amazement, the *HMS Rainbow* was gone.

And the *Gruel* was still in its place, near Birch Point.

Sarah saw Betsey and waved. "What has happened? Do you know? When did the *Rainbow* leave?"

"My pa just got back from the Point. He said the British sailors on the *Gruel* lowered their boats and escaped to the *Rainbow* in the middle of the night, and Admiral Collier sailed away."

"They just left?"

"The militia yesterday hit some marks. Several sailors required medical attention. They left Captain Proctor and his men on the *Gruel* well, but tied up. They destroyed some of the wood destined for France, and the captain's cabin, but that's all."

"They could have burned the *Gruel,* or the town. But they didn't."

"Captain Proctor said they'd planned to board the *Gruel* and sail off with her. They never expected she wouldn't have sails on board so they wouldn't be able to do that." Betsey laughed. "He said we should've heard how angry they were when they found out!"

"Yer father must be much relieved! And glad he thought of removing the sails!" said Sarah.

"Indeed. He is certainly glad they're gone, for whatever reason, and is just hoping they will not be back. They now know what cargo is within the *Gruel,* and will be looking for her when she sails for France."

"But at least for now the town is safe." Sarah felt as though they'd lived two months in the past two days. "Betsey, my mother's not well. I have to go home to Boothbay earlier than I'd expected."

"No! So soon!" Betsey stopped herself. "But I'm sorry your mother is ill."

"Jonathan told me when he brought the news that Admiral Collier had fired on Boothbay. I don't know what I'll find at home. Admiral Collier spared Wiscasset. He might not have spared Boothbay."

"When will you leave?"

"Later today, I hope, if Jonathan feels the *Rainbow* is safely to sea."

"Write to me, Sarah. And visit when you can."

"Aye. For sure I will, Betsey. And let us hope these dreadful war days are over soon, so letters and visits can be more easily exchanged."

The girls hugged each other, and Sarah ran down to where Jonathan usually left his skiff. In wartime running didn't seem as dreadful a thing to do as it had only weeks before.

Chapter 36

Malcolm's Pain

For a moment Rory thought he must be mistaken. Perhaps it wasn't his cousin.

Then he was sure.

Malcolm lay in the shadows, his body almost touching those of men on either side of him. So close Rory couldn't tell whose dark blood it was that soaked the straw beneath them. His left shoulder was twisted, and a bone was visible through the blood and muscle. Blood from a deep gash over his left eye covered half of his face, and dripped down onto his shoulder and into the straw.

"Malcolm! It's me. Rory."

Around them men were moaning and crying. Fifteen feet away Rory saw several men holding another down as a doctor sawed the man's leg off just above the knee.

"The pain … the pain …" Malcolm moved slightly, and moaned.

"I'll find someone who can help you." Rory went inside the barn and asked the first woman he saw, who was cleaning the leg wound of another soldier. "Please. My cousin is outside. He's in bad pain."

She looked up at Rory, her eyes weary and sad. "I'm sorry. I'll get to him when I can. But there are so many who need help, and so few of us. We have nothing for pain but some whiskey. Perhaps you can find some for him. I'm sorry. There are so many ..." She went back to sponging the blood off the soldier.

Rory asked everyone he could find. Most were women who'd traveled with their husbands to help with cooking and laundry. They had no special training in medicine.

One young woman was crying over the body of her husband.

Rory saw three men he thought might be doctors, but all three were amputating limbs. He didn't want them near Malcolm.

The smell of the blood and the wounded, and their cries of pain, filled the air as the sounds of the battlefield had filled his mind earlier that day.

Outside, he found Ethan waiting. "You stayed!"

"It was your cousin calling you, wasn't it," said Ethan.

"Aye."

"How is he?"

"He needs whiskey, for pain, and at least a clean bandage for his head. I can't find anyone to help. Ethan, I don't know what to do! I've never nursed anyone. Someone has to help him!"

"Stay with him. I'll find something for bandaging. And I think old Nathaniel has hidden some whiskey away in our hut. Do what you can until I return."

"Ethan. Thank you."

"I'll be back as soon as I can. You help Malcolm."

Rory nodded. Inside one of the supply wagons he found a pan no one was using.

He filled the pan at the creek that ran through camp and returned. Then he tore off a piece of his shirt off to use as a cloth.

"Malcolm, I'm going to start with your head and clean off the blood. My friend Ethan's trying to find a bandage. Maybe we can stop the bleeding."

"Pain ..." Malcolm murmured. He was barely conscious.

"Ethan's trying to find something for the pain." Rory tried not to look at Malcolm's shoulder. He knelt behind Malcolm's head and concentrated on carefully dipping the linen into the cold water and cleaning the blood away from Malcolm's face, and head, and neck. The wound was deeper than he'd thought, and went into Malcolm's eye socket.

Rory steadied his hand and focused on what he was doing, not on what the injury might mean. The blood was starting to clot. That must be good. Malcolm didn't seem to be losing as much blood as he had earlier.

The soldier on Malcolm's right who'd been moaning constantly became quiet. Rory glanced at him, hoping he'd fallen asleep. But he was dead.

Rory'd recognized the look of death immediately. Twenty-four hours ago he wouldn't have. Now death was all too familiar.

"I have rum. And part of a blanket for a bandage." Ethan was back. "The blanket's pretty clean, and I only tore off part, so Finnegan in the next hut won't hardly notice. And Nathaniel was snoring. He'll never know who stole his stash of rum."

"Thank you, Ethan!" Rory couldn't help smiling at his friend.

"May I help?"

"Help me hold his head a bit."

Ethan held Malcolm as Rory wound the piece of homespun blanket, covering his cousin's head wound and eye.

"Good job. He doesn't seem to be bleeding there anymore."

"No," said Rory. "Malcolm? Here's rum, for your pain. Can you swallow?"

Malcolm opened his mouth a little; Ethan held his head up, and Rory poured a few drops in. But raising his cousin's head clearly increased the pain in his shoulder.

Malcolm opened the eye not covered by the bandage. "What time is it? This night has lasted forever."

"It's morning now. Foggy, as always by the river, just like at home, but a couple of hours past dawn," said Rory.

"Did you fight? Did you have your battle?" Malcolm looked up at Rory. His words were hard to understand.

"Not yet, Malcolm. I haven't fought yet. You fought for both of us."

Chapter 37
Journey to Boothbay

Jonathan persuaded Sarah to wait one more day before they returned to Boothbay.

"What if Admiral Collins is waiting just down river? Or what if he decides to trick us, and return to Wiscasset? We have to allow another day, Sarah."

Sarah paced the floor and complained, but then Mr. Parsons, overhearing their plans, decided the militia should be involved. "You two should not be allowed to row twelve miles to Boothbay on your own when we know the British fired on the town. You don't know what you might find there. You might need reinforcements." He organized several boatloads of men to accompany them.

"You're going with a flotilla!" said Mrs. Biddle. "My dear Sarah, you'll be like a queen, returning with a retinue!"

"I don't need a retinue," said Sarah. "I just want to get home to Mother to see how she is. And how my town is." Privately, though, Sarah was glad there would be others with them. What if the town had been burned? What if people were injured? Or worse?

If that had happened, the more people and vessels to help, the better. Should major problems await them in Boothbay, she and Jonathan alone would not be able to do much with only four hands and one small skiff.

Mrs. Biddle was pleased to have the time to bake scones for Mrs. Campbell. "Even if she's feeling poorly, I'm sure she'll be able to eat a scone or two," Mrs. Biddle declared, and she helped pack even more mint leaves in Sarah's now bulging sack. Betsey added three parsnips from the Parsons' garden "because I've heard it's hard to grow root vegetables down on that rocky shore," and Sarah was glad to be bringing treasures of value back to Boothbay.

Even if Mother's stomach was not well, she knew Uncle Andra and Hugh would make short work of parsnips and scones.

"Do write, dear," said Mrs. Biddle, holding one of her black bordered handkerchiefs to her eye as Sarah finally left with Jonathan. "My little house will seem so quiet without you. Do consider coming back to Wiscasset, if your mother is well enough. You will always be welcome."

"Thank you, Mrs. Biddle," Sarah called back to her.

The sumac downriver was bright red, and yellows and oranges stained the leaves of maples and oaks alongside the pines and spruce trees lining the banks of the Sheepscot. Swallows had already flown south, and geese were honking and practicing formations for their own journeys. It had been almost eight weeks since Rory and Sarah had left Boothbay in Jonathan's skiff, heading for Wiscasset.

The journey was pleasant, despite Sarah's worry about what they might find in Boothbay. The men in the four boats called out to each other, pointing out landmarks and seals, osprey nests high in pine trees, or places that each remembered from past trips down the Sheepscot.

"If only all is well in Boothbay," Sarah repeated over and over to herself. "If only Mother is well, and the town safe."

No sign of any problem was visible on Southport Island. The one home they could see from the river looked as it always did.

They anchored in Campbell's Cove. If aid was needed in another part of the harbor, the boats could be taken there.

The McFarlands' house was the closest. Muskets at the ready, the men marched ahead.

Mr. McFarland answered their knocks. "Is there a meeting of the militia hereabouts I haven't been notified about?"

"We heard Admiral Collier was firing on Boothbay. He then came to Wiscasset. We came to see if any aid was needed here," said Mr. Parsons.

"Well, bless you all! We did have some excitement here a few days ago. Hello, there, Sarah! Welcome home. Your ma's gonna be real pleased to see you."

"Is everyone all right? Did Admiral Collier burn any houses?" asked Sarah, pushing herself through the crowd of men so she could talk with Mr. McFarland.

"The admiral had that in mind, I think. He fired some cannon balls up this way. With the drought we've had, some marsh grasses did catch fire, so that was a bit of a problem, but, luckily, none of those fires were near houses. Then he sent some of his men to land, in two of his longboats. We figured he was after the last of our animals."

"What happened then?" asked Mr. Parsons.

Mr. McFarland was clearly enjoying having an audience for his story. "There was a bit of musket fire, on both sides, you know. Now, Joseph Strong, from over to the east side of the harbor, he did get grazed a bit on his right arm. He's mending all right, as I hear it. But that made his neighbors mighty angry, so they used up most of the ammunition we'd been saving." Mr. McFarland shook his head. "Scared those English fellows right back into their little boats. But two of 'em was a bit slow, and we got 'em afore they could get back to sea."

"You captured two British sailors?"

"Yup. We haven't got a jail in Boothbay, so we've got 'em tied up in the old Elderkin place. You know where that is, Sarah."

Sarah nodded. "Where's Mr. Elderkin?"

"He left us for a better place about a month ago, I'm afraid, Sarah. But his house is pretty sturdy, and we've got the Seacoast Defense standing guard there twenty-four hours a day. Glad you fellows are here, though. Be happy to have you take those two sailors back to Wiscasset with you. We've got no use for 'em here in Boothbay."

"Then everyone here's all right?" asked Sarah, again.

"Everyone but Joseph Strong, who's got the sore arm. Nothing too exciting going on here." Mr. McFarland smiled and leaned back against his door, and the Wiscasset militia grinned back at him and shook their heads.

"Guess we've got prisoners to take back up river," said Mr. Parsons.

"I'm going home!" said Sarah, and she ran the rest of the way.

Mother was alone, sitting by the table. "Sarah! Oh, Sarah, dear!"

Sarah ran into her arms. It felt so good to be home. Then she backed away. "But, Mother, how do ye feel?"

"I feel just fine. Don't I look well?"

"Uncle Andra told Jonathan I should come home because you were poorly. Your stomach was giving you problems." Sarah looked at her mother again. "But ye look fine to me. Somehow ye've even gained a bit of weight, despite the shortages."

Mother burst into laughter. "Men! I cannot believe Andra called ye home because of my stomach! Oh, but Sarah, I am so very glad to see ye. I want to hear everything about Wiscasset. And it was almost time fer ye to be comin' home in any case. It's almost October. There's not a thing wrong with me. I just didn't want to tell anyone until I was sure all was as it should be." She looked at Sarah and smiled. "Sarah, my stomach is quite fine. Yer going to have a little brother or sister."

OCTOBER, 1777

Chapter 38
Between Battles

The British didn't attack again the next day, or the next, or the day after that.

With his captain's permission, Rory spent his days caring for his cousin. One of the doctors was able to pull Malcolm's arm and shoulder bones back into place, and set those that were broken. Unless gangrene set in, the prognosis for keeping the arm was good. It might not be able to move as it had in the past, but Malcolm, unlike many of his wounded comrades, would return home with all of his limbs.

The doctor was not as optimistic about his sight. "There's little can be done about nerves in the eyes, and those in your left eye have been torn. You're mending well, Malcolm, and rest will help, but I don't think you'll see out of that left eye again. Luckily," the doctor added, touching him gently on his good shoulder, "your right eye is fine. A man can see most everything he needs to see with one good eye."

Malcolm refused to accept the doctor's prognosis. "My eye will mend, just as my arm will," he said, over and over.

Rory wasn't as sure, but he was thankful Malcolm was alive. So many of the other injured soldiers had died. Malcolm was healing, and he wasn't blind, and hadn't lost his arm. He couldn't fight again, but he would live. It was a blessing.

Rumors were everywhere that the British Army was running low on food. Some American men left camp at night and watched for English soldiers roaming the countryside, foraging for food for themselves and their horses. Musket fire pierced the darkness every night, but no one spoke of it.

Several times each day one or more British or German soldiers walked into the American camp to surrender. The Americans had food.

What they didn't have was ammunition.

They'd used more than General Gates had anticipated during the battle they were now calling the Battle of Freeman's Farm. The general had sent messengers south to Albany, asking that civilians there melt any lead in their windows and cast it into musket balls for the army.

Every night he ordered his soldiers to line up the supply wagons on the road headed down the hill from the Heights and fill them with any ammunition, food, or other provisions the men couldn't carry. No one knew how many British soldiers General Burgoyne had in his camp, and General Gates remembered the retreat from Ticonderoga, when the Americans had left most of their supplies for the British because they couldn't carry them. If such a retreat should be necessary from Bemis Heights the Americans couldn't afford to lose any more supplies. Or leave anything useful to Burgoyne's troops.

"How can he ask us to prepare for retreat every night and then drill every day as though we were going to advance?" Ethan asked Malcolm. "Doesn't he believe we can win the battle to come?"

"General Gates stayed within the defenses during the Battle of Freeman's Farm. He wasn't on the field, like our other generals. Or like General Burgoyne, or General Fraser, or General von Riedesel. If he'd been there he'd have seen. Our men can do it, Rory. We just need one more chance. I may not be among them next time, but you will.

You'll see. We just need one more chance."

Every day the American soldiers worked on their fortifications, and every night the men slept with their muskets at the ready. Another battle was inevitable. The only question was when.

"Will General Gates ask our unit to fight next time?" asked Ethan, when he and Rory were quietly waiting for orders one morning.

"He must," said Rory. "Perhaps it was by chance he didn't call on us the last time. He didn't call on half the regular army units. Most likely we were next in line when night fell and the battle ended. That won't happen again, I'd wager."

"We know more about battles now," said Ethan, looking toward where the new graves and the hospital were.

"We know more about what battles do to men," corrected Rory. "We haven't yet fought in one."

"This is how new nations are born," said Ethan. "This is why we're here."

"Is it?" said Rory. "I'd like to think that. But I'm beginning to believe many of us came for the excitement, and some for the glory."

Ethan laughed. "If it's glory someone's wanting, they'd best search somewhere else. Glory's in history books. What's here is stinking latrines and homesick men and soldiers like Malcolm, who'll be reminded every day of his life about what happened at Freeman's Farm. "

"Aye; you're right. But maybe new nations are born of all that," Rory said quietly. "I've never seen braver men than I have here. They'll be the makings of a grand new country. If we win."

Chapter 39
Sarah's Place

"Has any word come from Rory or Malcolm?" asked Sarah after she and Mother had gotten caught up on events in Boothbay and Wiscasset. "I think of them every day."

"Aye. As do we," said Mother. "And keep them in our prayers, both spoken and thought. I still canna believe our Rory was headstrong enough to take off and leave like that." She shook her head. "So young, and so far away from us. If, indeed, he got to York County to enlist as he intended."

"He was so excited and determined, Mother. I met the man who told him the army at Ticonderoga needed reinforcements. He seemed fair and honest. I trust he was giving Rory good information. I heard later at least one other man from Wiscasset went with him. I've not heard of word coming back from either of them, but ye know how difficult it is. Few ships travel north in these times, and fewer people travel north by land."

"Indeed. We've heard nothing from Malcolm, and he's been gone three times as long as Rory."

"We heard Fort Ticonderoga had fallen," Sarah pointed out.

"Jonathan brought that news. But no news of whether there were casualties." Mother shook her head. "It would be easier to be there, I think, fighting, and knowing what was happening from day to day than sitting and waiting, imagining the worst and hoping for the best. And now to have *two* young men gone."

"Rory should be back by the end of the year. He said the York militia was only asking men to sign on for three months," said Sarah.

"Perhaps. But in this war rules change, and are often ignored. Rules say you must be sixteen to enlist, after all," said Mother. "And since Ticonderoga fell, we don't know where either of them are, nor how long it would take Rory to journey home, even if his enlistment were up. So there's no sense counting days."

"Then we must stay busy, and think of happier things," said Sarah.

"Aye; I agree," said Mother, getting up from her bench. "Let me show ye one of my projects since ye've been in Wiscasset. I unraveled an old wool shirt of Rory's, since he is not here to use it, and I knit a fishing net from it. Hugh and your uncle have been using lanterns to attract fish to the beach at night. They've caught us enough to last a good part of winter. I've been smoking the fish out in the field, far enough from the house to keep the flies from the doorway. I'll show ye."

"When will the baby be coming?" asked Sarah, as they walked on a worn path through the low brambles. Leaves that had been yellow and red were now crumbling brown, and most had fallen in early morning frosts and northeast winds. Winds off the water were cold, and Sarah shivered remembering the frigid days of the winter before.

"It will be a winter baby," said Mother. "Most likely joining us in February."

"We'll need more cloths for clouts, and some clothing," Sarah said, thinking of Betsey's many younger brothers and sisters. "There are no sheep here for wool. Perhaps Betsey's family would have some to spare. They have so many children, Mother — eight of them! But only one still in clouts. There are a few sheep in Wiscasset. Some women are spinning and weaving."

"They are lucky," her mother nodded. "I don't like depending on others, but perhaps closer to the time ye could share our news with yer friend, and mention it would be a great kindness if they had a few clouts we could use. For the first months I'll bundle the little one up with Andra and me in our bed for warmth." She smiled at Sarah. "Hugh has said he will make a cradle. I believe at first he was quite taken aback at the idea of having a brother or sister twenty years younger than he is, but he's coming around. After all, he's old enough to be thinking of marriage himself. Perhaps someday soon he'll be needing the cradle himself."

"Does he have anyone in mind, do ye think?"

"Of late I've noticed him spending a good deal of time over near Ocean Point, near Patrick Pinkham's home. The Pinkhams have a daughter only a few years older than ye, do they not?"

"Their Hannah is sixteen, I believe," said Sarah. "She is very quiet; I hardly know her."

"Perhaps it's just a mother's thought, but I believe we may get to know Hannah better in the future." Mother stopped. "Here's where I'm drying fish."

In front of them was a high, slatted wooden rack on stone blocks. Under the racks were the smoking remnants of fires. And on the racks were gutted fish, covered with thin muslin. "Mother! Those are your petticoats on the fish!" Sarah said. "Whatever are you wearing under your skirts?"

"Who will know, but you and your uncle," said Mother. "When the fires are going, the gulls stay away because of the smoke. But we canna be here all the time, so the muslin helps. The fish smoke and dry in the sun. The process is helped by putting salt on the fish before we start the fires."

"But the flies!" Flies covered everything … muslin and fish alike. Sarah wrinkled her nose.

"Flies are a part of life. We will rinse the fish before we soak it and eat it in the winter in any case." Her mother turned back toward the house. "Now that yer here, ye can help with filling the boxes near the ocean with sea water so we can gather more salt. We have used more than usual, and I've found myself weary recently."

"Aye; of course, Mother," said Sarah. "That is why I'm here. To help."

Her mother smiled. "I'm glad yer home. Ye've grown up in the past months, Sarah. It'll be good to have another woman in the house when the child comes."

Chapter 40
Before the Battle

By October, frosts had forced morning fogs to give way to brisk clear air that reminded New Englanders at Bemis Heights of apple picking and cider making. It was the time of year to make certain cold cellars were filled with pumpkins and squash and turnips and carrots. Time to weave pine branches and hay around the base of homes to help keep out the chill of winter.

"Hate leaving my wife to do all that herself," Nathaniel said as he lay on his blanket in the dark one night before they'd fallen asleep. His musket was beside him, and his knapsack was his pillow. "Neighbors said they'd help out when I was gone, but they've got their own places, and everyone's time is stretched when winter's close upon us."

Seth nodded. "Hope heavy snows hold off until we're home. I don't look forward to crossing those Berkshires heading east in drifting snow."

They'd signed on for three months. Half that time was up.

"You know what some are calling this year?" Ira spoke up from the corner of the hut that had become his. "The year of the hangman."

"Why?" asked Ethan.

"Think of it," said Ira. "1777. Those three sevens look a lot like gibbets. By the British way of looking at it, we're all traitors, every one of us. We're rebelling against the king. We could all hang."

"All twelve thousand of us? And that's just here at the Heights," said Rory. "It would take a forest of trees to build that many gibbets!"

A couple of the men chuckled in the dark.

Ethan shook his head. "It's already October. I'll not lose sleep over some superstition." He shifted his position on the hard earth, trying to find a comfortable spot.

"But what if we don't win the war? After all, we gave up at Ticonderoga, and were defeated at Hubbardton. I heard General Washington's Army lost a battle at a place called Brandywine in Pennsylvania last month," said Nathaniel. "The British now hold New York and Philadelphia. Congress has had to move to Lancaster, Pennsylvania. Doesn't sound good to me."

"But our forces killed and captured all those loyalists near Bennington!" said Ethan.

"We did. But there are still plenty of Germans around, even though some have deserted. And that last battle right here, at Freeman's Farm? What did that really accomplish? We lost men, and they lost men. And where are our armies now? Right where we were before the battle." Nathaniel sounded weary.

"We'll fight again," said Ethan. "No doubt."

"No doubt," agreed Seth. "And next time we'll win."

"We'd best," said Nathaniel, "I don't like hearing that Year of the Hangman talk."

They were all silent.

"We have faith in ourselves, don't we?" said Rory. "We came here to fight for the freedom to make our own laws; not have them dictated by men three thousand miles across the sea. We won't leave until we do that. We won't be like those men from New Hampshire who went home before the battle because their enlistment period was up."

"I'm not leaving now," said Nathaniel. "But if we're sleeping in these cold huts in the snow in six weeks, I might give you another answer."

Cold rain started as they fell asleep. It pelted Bemis Heights all through the night. The morning of October 7 dawned bright, but the ground was muddy and the men's clothing was damp and chill from sleeping on the ground. Trees stood dark against the sky, their branches naked, like the bones of skeletons.

Rory woke early. He touched Ethan's shoulder. "I'm going to see Malcolm before they start us digging latrines or put us to some other task."

Outside the hut, he stopped. Soldiers were running, not walking, to their duties. He remembered when that had happened before.

He stuck his head back inside. "Friends, this may be the day we've been waiting for."

Throughout the American camp soldiers were waiting and watching. Messengers ran between the officers' quarters. Scouts were sent out; some returned and went directly to General Gates' headquarters. But no troops were ordered out.

Rory received permission to visit Malcolm briefly but to "return directly."

Malcolm's arm was beginning to heal, although both his wounds still throbbed. "Can you hear the troops?" said Rory. "Today may be the day of the battle. Our militia unit is under General Paterson now, the same as your old regiment."

Malcolm was silent for a long minute. "Rory, yer a soldier. Do what ye must. We're fighting for a good cause. I believed that when I enlisted, and I believe that now."

"Those Brits cost ye an eye, and part use of yer arm, and killed so

And then, finally, General Paterson's forces: four regiments of Massachusetts regulars and two units of Massachusetts militia, including Colonel Storer's men from York.

They followed a narrow wagon road about a mile through the woods. With every step they marched the musket fire sounded closer.

A man marching behind Rory softly recited the Lord's Prayer.

They tried to stay in lines, but other units were in the woods, and the closer they got to the fighting, the more men they saw, wounded, dead, and fighting within the woods.

At the far end of the trees they reached what only that morning had been a large field of corn. Rory tightened his grip on his musket as he stared at the horror in front of him. Bodies of dead and dying red-coated British soldiers and a few blue-coated German soldiers were strewn across the field, mingled with mud from the past night's rain and blood and trampled yellow stalks of grain. Beyond the bodies were more wounded men, British, American, and German. And men of all three countries. Running.

Despite the confusion, the troops were running forward, toward the right. Rory ran with them. At first he ran alongside men in his company, but soon he recognized no one near him. He glimpsed the face of one man who belonged to the Canadian regiment camped near his.

It didn't matter. The focus was on the enemy.

Blood. Red leaves. Pieces of flesh. Red uniforms. Dead horses. He stepped over bodies. Weapons. Tree stumps.

Cannons kept pounding. The field was slippery with blood and mud.

Through another wooded area lay a second field of devastation. His legs kept moving. Ahead was a hill, the top protected with barricades, much like the ones at Bemis Heights. But these were British defenses. Americans were charging it, and bodies, British and

American, lay on the slope leading up to where British soldiers were frantically loading and reloading their guns.

The ground shook with the pounding of the cannons ahead. The air was filled with the dark smoke and flames of cannon fire and the smell of sulfur.

It was as he had always pictured Hell.

The whole hill seemed to be covered in flames, like in his worst nightmares. Rory almost stopped. But he couldn't even scream. His mind went blank, but his body kept moving. On his left he saw a British officer on a large gray horse, riding back and forth, rallying his men. As he watched, the man crumpled onto the horse's neck. Two of his men appeared, helped him balance on the horse, and led him away.

Suddenly General Arnold rode in front of Rory, almost knocking him down. "Follow me! Follow me!" he shouted.

"This way!" said the soldier next to Rory. He was pulling a small British cannonade. "Help pull!"

Rory took the end of a rope and helped pull the small cannon up the hill, passing other soldiers with small artillery and muskets as they ran.

The British had deserted their canons. They must be retreating. Rory tried to think, but his mind was too filled with sounds and images. Men stumbling. Falling.

At the top of the hill the smoke cleared for a moment. The field was littered with bodies, some red coated, some blue, and every color American uniform. The field was surrounded by woods, and cannons, and soldiers.

How did anyone know where to shoot? Men were everywhere.

A shot passed by Rory's shoulder. He turned, without thinking, and fired. A red-coated soldier ten feet away fell.

Rory loaded again and watched. Glints of red and steel shone between the trees. As soon as he saw an image clear enough, he fired in that direction, and reloaded. Over and over. Muskets were not accurate, but with luck he could hit someone. Without luck he could scare someone into moving somewhere else, away from the cannons.

He forgot to feel the ground shaking under his feet, and didn't see the smoke or the fire from the guns. All he saw was one group of trees. And the color red.

The fighting went on until nightfall.

All that night camp followers and soldiers on both sides removed the wounded to the British and American hospital areas. Bodies of the dead British were stripped for much-needed weapons, shoes, and clothing.

After it was all over, very late that night, Rory whispered to Ethan, "How did you feel? Were you scared? Did you see the British and the Germans running?"

"At first I was scared," said Ethan. "Then I was too busy to be afraid." He paused. "I'm glad I came, and fought. But, you're my friend, Rory. I can tell you. I've tested myself, and I've proved I can be a soldier. No man can say I can't, or I won't. But I'll be glad to be going home." He paused in the darkness of their hut. "And you?"

"It's not simple, Ethan. I don't know what I want to do. But I think my nightmares are over. I've lived through worse than I ever dreamed."

It wasn't until the next morning that they learned Colonel Storer was one of those who had fallen. He would not be leading his regiment back to York County, Maine.

NOVEMBER, 1777

Chapter 42
Surrender

On the night of the day after the battle General Burgoyne began moving what was left of his army north, believing he could retreat back to Fort Ticonderoga, seventy miles north, and then on to Canada.

His men were exhausted, his supplies low, and heavy cold rain made the muddy road almost impassable for his carts and wagons. Soldiers from the American Army followed his troops. Some units crossed the Hudson and got ahead of the British soldiers, blocking their retreat.

As the rest of Gates' army followed they found what the British could not carry: wounded and dying soldiers left in their hospital, wagons, carcasses of horses, tents, and even ammunition.

On October 11 an entire picket guard of Germans deserted and came over to the American line. The British had little food, and since the path to the Hudson River was blocked by the Americans, they now had little water.

On October 17 it was all over.

"One for the history books," Seth said so many times that one of the other men cuffed him.

Agreement had been reached. Gentleman Johnny Burgoyne and his troops had agreed to surrender.

It was the first time a British Army had ever been defeated. Burgoyne had started from Quebec in June with ten thousand men. Now he had fewer than six thousand.

The American camp had moved from Bemis Heights to the south bank of Fish Creek, where they'd followed the British Army.

"How do you think those British soldiers feel?" said Rory. "They came all the way to this country, and fought, and now they've lost, and they're going to have to march all the way to Boston."

"I heard our General Gates and their General Burgoyne knew each other as boys in England. They were both in the British Army when they were your age, Rory," Seth added. "General Gates found that life not to his liking, so he sailed to America and made a new start."

"And now they've met again." Ethan looked at Rory. "If we meet again in thirty years, I hope we won't be on opposite sides."

Rory laughed. "That won't happen. Not in America." He hesitated. "The British officer I saw shot on the battlefield was General Fraser, the Scottish general who was so well-liked."

"He was killed by Tim Murphy, an Irish rifleman from Pennsylvania. Funny, isn't it? Irish and Scots, still fighting, even in America," said Seth.

"No," said Rory. "An American patriot shot a British officer. No matter where we came from, here in the United States we're all Americans."

The American Army lined both sides of the road, muskets in hand, and watched with respect as the prisoners of war marched by. General Burgoyne rode, elegant in his red dress uniform glittering with gold embroidery. He was greeted by General Gates, who wore a simple blue coat.

Both generals dismounted. Burgoyne handed Gates his sword, in the classic European tradition of surrender. Gates returned it.

170

Marching by the generals were brigade after brigade, regiment after regiment, of British and German soldiers. They wore uniforms of red or blue or green, dirty and ragged from a hard campaign in the wilds of New York. They stood proud. But they had no weapons. Their muskets and bayonets now belonged to the Americans.

Despite the somber occasion, many Continentals smiled as they saw dozens of German soldiers marching by holding small animals and birds – raccoons, squirrels, crows, and even skunks – that they had tamed as pets during their months in the forests of New York.

Most of the Americans who watched, knapsacks, cartridge boxes, and powder horns slung over their shoulders and hands on their muskets or rifles, did not wear uniforms. Most wore the clothing they wore at home, on farms, in small towns, on the frontier, in cities, or on fishing boats. Some were as young as twelve, and some as old as seventy. A few women who had followed the men, or who lived nearby, stood with them. Whoever they were, whatever their rank, and wherever they came from, they, too, stood tall.

As the soldiers marched the American fifers and drummers played "Yankee Doodle." The British had first written that song to make fun of American soldiers during the French and Indian wars. Now the Americans claimed it as their own.

After the ceremony was over and the troops had left, the only question for the York men was, "When can we leave for home?"

"Snow is already flirting, and we have the Berkshires to cross," was said too many times a day to count.

Malcolm was healing, which was well, since the army's field hospital was being moved to Albany.

"Do ye truly feel strong enough to walk?" asked Rory. "The British soldiers only have to march two hundred miles to Boston. Boothbay's another hundred and fifty miles past that."

"Aye. Sure and it is," Malcolm said. "And I'll be able." Then he admitted, "There are times I'll be in need of your shoulder to learn on. Without a shoulder I might walk into trees on some of those rough trails. I'm not yet used to seeing out of only one eye."

Rory realized the eye was not Malcolm's only challenge. Malcolm's injuries had taken much of his strength along with his sight.

There was no question of Malcolm's returning to his regiment. But how was he to get home to Boothbay?

Ethan and Rory spent more and more time together. Their months as militia men were ending.

Malcolm's regiment was scheduled to leave in two days. And the York Regiment, without Colonel Storer, was heading east at the same time.

"I know what you want to do, Rory," Ethan said quietly one day. "I can help you. You don't have to worry."

"What do ye mean?" asked Rory.

"I've asked the others, and we'll do it. We have two wagons, and Malcolm can walk part way. He's a Maine man, and a patriot, and he's your cousin. We'll take him home, Rory. We'll leave you free."

Rory looked at him. "How did ye know?"

"How could I walk next to you and sleep next to you and fight next to you for three months and not know what you've been thinking, Rory Campbell? Did you think I was daft?"

"I've spoken to his captain. They'll take me."

"That doesn't surprise me," said Ethan. "You'll be a courageous soldier. You'll fight for all of us, and make us proud. Does Malcolm know?"

"Not yet. I'll talk with him. He'll understand." Rory laughed quietly. "It's Mother who won't understand. But she'll have Malcolm to fuss over, so that'll be some help."

"Where will you be going?"

"I'll be taking Malcolm's place, his captain said. The British have now taken Philadelphia. We'll be heading to Pennsylvania, to join General Washington's troops in their winter quarters, just outside of Philadelphia. A place called Valley Forge."

DECEMBER, 1777

Chapter 43
Boothbay, Late December, 1777

Bitter northeast winds had howled for weeks around the little house in Boothbay. Even the spruce branches woven high on the outside walls and the fire burning constantly in the fireplace couldn't keep them truly warm.

Sarah and her mother wore most of the clothes they owned, and wrapped quilts around themselves when the clothes were not enough to ward off the cold.

They'd long since used up the mint Mrs. Biddle had sent from her garden, and longed for that fresh summer smell. Instead, they sipped plain water, heated from melted snow, to warm themselves. Here by the ocean snow wasn't as deep as it was inland, in places like Wiscasset, but there was enough for drinking and washing. Both the pump and stream had been frozen since mid-October. Hugh and Uncle Andra kept the woodpile high and the fire burning.

They only went out when it was necessary, using chamber pots and emptying them once a day in the frozen privy. Sarah looked often at the pine cradle Hugh had made that waited next to the fireplace.

If only the baby would come easily, and be well. February winds and weather would be worse than December's, and although several Boothbay women had said they would come when it was Mother's time, Sarah worried that icy winter storms might

prevent their arriving in time to be of help. Mother had explained what help she would need should that happen, but it would be Sarah's first experience at a birth, and she very much hoped for the presence of another woman.

Uncle Andra was also nervous. It seemed as though three times a day he asked Mother if she felt well. Hugh said little, but Sarah often thought she saw him looking at Mother's growing shape with awe.

Through their concern, Mother stayed calm and reassuring. Betsey and her mother had send a basket full of clouts and small warm dresses and even two blankets and hats made for tiny babies, and she delighted in looking at them.

"Will the baby really be that tiny?" asked Sarah.

"You were," said Mother. "And no baby was more beautiful."

So together they waited for the winds to stop howling and the next member of their family to join them. Every day they prayed for Malcolm and for Rory, and tried not to think about their loved ones who were absent.

In November Jonathan had brought a letter from Mrs. Biddle, full of excitement. Her dear nephew, the Reverend Bailey, had been called to a new parish in Nova Scotia, and she was going with him as soon as they could find a ship to take them. She wished Sarah and her family well, and sent her teapot and teacups as a gift for Sarah.

On this December day, Hugh and Uncle Andra were at the McFarland's house for a Seacoast Defense meeting.

"I sometimes think those meetings are a bit of an excuse for the men to get out of the house in the wintertime and share some rum or cider," said Mother, unraveling one of Uncle Andra's socks that had several holes. It was too worn to darn; she was going to reknit it. "Men folk get even more restless than we do, Sarah."

Their heavy door banged open, bringing in wisps of snow and

cold wind and stamping feet.

They both looked up. "Malcolm!" Mother dropped her sock, and ran to embrace him, as Malcolm stood awkwardly between Father and Hugh. Another young man stood behind them in the doorway.

"Please, come in, so we can latch the door against the wind," said Sarah to the newcomer, getting up. "Do sit down. Now, Malcolm! Welcome home!"

"Jonathan found these two in Wiscasset and brought them to us," said Father. "They'd gotten as far as McFarland's, and we left Jonathan there to get warm, but came here as soon as we could."

Malcolm was thin, and what was left of his uniform was worn and faded. His left hand clutched a piece of blanket around his shoulders to keep him warm. His arm was held at an odd angle. A white bandage wrapped around his head and covered his left eye. But his broad smile was unmistakable.

"Come, Malcolm, you've been on a long journey. Sit at the table, and tell us everything." Mother pulled out a chair, and almost pushed Malcolm down into it. She stood in back of him, looked at Uncle Andra, smiling, and yet shaking her head in sadness as she looked at Malcolm's injuries.

"And who are you?" Sarah asked the other man.

Uncle Andra interrupted.

"This is Ethan Chase, of Wiscasset, Sarah. He enlisted with our Rory and was with him on the journey to New York. They met up with Malcolm at the Battles of Saratoga, and now he's helped bring our Malcolm home to us."

Mother, her eyes damp, looked at Malcolm, and then at Ethan. "And Rory? You didn't bring Rory home? Then Rory is...?"

"No, Ma'am! Rory's fine, so far as I know. After Malcolm was injured, Rory enlisted and took his place in the 11th Massachusetts. Last time I seen him he was marching off with his regiment to join

General Washington's Army in Pennsylvania."

Mother sat down again, shaking her head.

"Rory always did want to be a soldier," said Sarah. "I guess he got his wish."

"He'll be a good soldier," said Malcolm. "Ethan here was good enough to bring me all the way back to ye. He can tell ye all about Rory." He turned to Mother. "I'm fine, but a little weak still from injuries. And unless my good eye deceives me … am I right in supposing I'm to have another brother soon?"

"Or perhaps a sister!" said Uncle Andra. "Yer home in time to be part of all the excitement, Malcolm."

"Now, Ethan and Malcolm, warm yourselves, and tell us all about Rory, and the battles, and how you got yourself back to Maine," said Mother.

"I'll get ye some hot cider," said Sarah. "We've been saving it for an occasion."

"We'll all have some to celebrate," said Uncle Andra. "This is indeed a special day."

"And we'll drink a toast to Rory, somewhere in Pennsylvania," said Malcolm. "May he serve our country well, be in good health, and come home to us safely when the war is won."

"And may the war be over soon," said Sarah, raising her cup. "Most of all. So all men can be back with their families, as Malcolm is with ours, and we can live in peace."

HISTORICAL NOTES & QUESTIONS

General Burgoyne's surrender at Saratoga marked the first time a British army
    had fallen to that of a colony. Often called the turning point of the American Revolutionary War, it was a major reason France was convinced to become an American ally in 1778. But the war was far from over.

    Approximately 1,000 Massachusetts men from the District of Maine were among those with General Washington in his encampment at Valley Forge, Pennsylvania, during the winter of 1777-1778. In June the British withdrew from Philadelphia and Congress returned. But the war moved south, as British forces captured Savannah, Georgia. In 1779 Spain also declared war on Britain, fighting moved to the frontier, and Washington's army spent the hardest winter of the war at Morristown, New Jersey.

    1780 began with two major British victories in the south: the siege of Charleston, followed by its capture, and General Gates' (now commanding the Southern Continental Army) defeat at Camden, North Carolina. In the fall, shockingly, American General Benedict Arnold was discovered offering to surrender West Point to the British, and fled to the enemy's side. Patriot forces won the Battle of

King's Mountain in South Carolina. By 1781 the Continental Army was weary. The Pennsylvania and New Jersey lines mutinied. Battles in North and South Carolina continued, and the Spanish took Pensacola, Florida. Finally, in August, General Washington and the French coordinated an attack on Yorktown, Virginia, and laid siege to the city where British General Cornwallis' troops were waiting for supplies and reinforcements. Although small battles were fought on the frontier for eighteen more months, and British forces did not leave New York City until November of 1783, the War for American Independence was over on October 19, 1781 when Cornwallis surrendered at Yorktown.

Who fought on the American side during the Revolution?
The men who fought on the American side of the Revolutionary War came from all thirteen colonies (which during the war became known as states), from Vermont (which was then a self-declared separate country), and from Canada. Individual men from many European countries came to the new world to fight as well. After France was convinced to support the new United States government, soldiers and sailors from those countries also joined the American side.

Although there were men (and a few women) who fought independently, joining in for short periods, particularly when battles were near their homes, most of those fighting on the American side were either enlisted in the Continental Army, which was authorized by the Continental Congress, or were members of local or state militias which owed allegiance to their states, not to Congress.

All able-bodied men between the ages of sixteen and sixty were expected to serve in local militias to protect their homes, as the Seacoast Defense did along the coast of Maine (which was then a part of Massachusetts). When the Army needed additional forces, which happened often, state militias would enlist members for short periods, usually two to six months, to go where they were needed. At the end of their enlistment period militiamen were free to return home, although they could be forced to remain and serve under dire circumstances. Militias supplied their own weapons, clothing, and supplies or were given such by their states. Soldiers in the army (often referred to as "regulars") were supposed to be given these things, and soldiers in both the Army and militia were promised pay. Unfortunately, because the Continental Army was underfunded, they did not always receive the supplies or pay owed them.

Militias in many parts of New England elected their own officers, who were usually local men they trusted and knew well. They obeyed these officers first, and occasionally there were conflicts with the Army officers planning battle maneuvers. For that reason, and because individual militias participated for only short periods as part of the army, regular army officers had mixed feelings about the militia. They needed their help, but could not always count on them to respond as they were directed.

A man might enlist in the army, leave, and then perhaps enlist for varying periods in several militias, perhaps even in different states, during the course of the war. Because record keeping was sometimes poor, particularly in the militias, it is hard to know exactly who fought, and where. Historians generally agree that over 200,000 men fought on the Patriot side at some time during the American Revolution.

About half of the American soldiers were new immigrants, most of them from Ireland, Scotland, England, or Germany.

Some Native American nations fought for the British, and some for the Americans. Black Americans were also divided. Free African Americans from northern states enlisted in the Continental Army, and some masters in the northern states promised their slaves freedom if they fought in the war. Most of one Rhode Island regiment was made up of free African Americans, slaves, and Native Americans. The slaves were freed after their enlistments were up.

But the British offered freedom to any slave who left his master and fought for them, so many slaves in the south left their masters and fought with the British, hoping they were also fighting for their freedom.

Were the characters in Contrary Winds real people?
All the military leaders at Saratoga and in the Maine militia are historical figures, as are Admiral Collier and his men on the frigate *HMS Rainbow.* Some of the other people in Wiscasset – Reverend Bailey, Mr. Parsons, Mr. Rice, Captain Proctor of the *Gruel,* and the *Gruel*'s cook who was the first to call for help, are also real people.

The other characters in *Contrary Winds,* including the Campbell family (who are based on a Scottish family who lived in Boothbay) and Ethan Chase and Mrs. Biddle, are fictional, but represent men and women who lived in the District of Maine in 1777.

A special note to those who know the State of Maine as it is now: what was the city of Falmouth in 1777 is now Portland, South Portland, and the town of Falmouth. The area of Boothbay where the Campbells lived is now called Boothbay Harbor. Townsend Harbor is now Boothbay Harbor. Campbell's Cove was dammed in 1879 and is now West Harbor Pond. Jeremy Squam Island is now Westport Island.

Did these events really take place? Why was the Battle of Saratoga important?
The historical events portrayed in this book – the British seizure (and loss) of the mast ship *Gruel* in Wiscasset and the Battles at Saratoga

– really happened. The militia and army units described were a part of those military engagements.

The Battle of Saratoga was a major turning point in the Revolutionary War. Winning it proved to France that the United States could be a worthy ally, and as a result the French sent much-needed naval forces to back up the Continental Army. At the same time, the coalition of regular army units and militias who traveled to Saratoga and fought there proved to the Congress and to the officers of the Continental Army itself that the American people would seriously back the military effort needed to win the war.

For more information on the Battle of Saratoga, and to find out about visiting the battlefield itself, see the website http://www.nps.gov/sara

What about the time periods? Were all the events in Maine and New York happening at the same time, as described in Contrary Winds?
Closely, but not exactly. In order to tell both Sarah's story, the story of the Revolution on the home front and the local militias in northeastern New England, and Rory's story, of a militiaman traveling to and participating in the battles which we refer to collectively as the Battle of Saratoga, I took some liberty with slowing down events in Maine and speeding up those in New York State. The actual dates are:

The 3rd York Militia left Maine August 14, 1777

The *HMS Rainbow* attacked Boothbay September 8

General Gates' Army arrived at Stillwater September 9

HMS Rainbow sailed up the Sheepscot and sailors boarded the *Gruel* at Wiscasset September 10

HMS Rainbow departed September 11

General Gates' army moved to Bemis Heights September 12

The first Battle of Saratoga, known as Freeman's Farm, was September 19

The second Battle of Saratoga, known as Bemis Heights, was October 7

General Burgoyne's surrender was October 17

The 3rd York Militia officially disbanded November 30, 1777

Other Books by Lea Wait

Historical Novels for ages 8 and Up

Stopping to Home
Seaward Born
Wintering Well
Finest Kind
Uncertain Glory
Contrary Winds
For Freedom Alone

Contemporary Mystery for ages 8 and Up

Pizza to Die For

Nonfiction

Living and Writing on the Coast of Maine

Mysteries for Adults

Death and a Pot of Chowder (written under name Cornelia Kidd)

Twisted Threads
Threads of Evidence
Thread and Gone

Dangling By a Thread
Tightening the Threads
Thread the Halls
Thread Herrings

Shadows at the Fair
Shadows on the Coast of Maine
Shadows on the Ivy
Shadows at the Spring Show
Shadows of a Down East Summer
Shadows on a Cape Cod Wedding
Shadows on a Maine Christmas
Shadows on a Morning in Maine

Made in the USA
Columbia, SC
17 August 2018